CELTIC
WONDER-TALES

CELTIC
WONDER-TALES

RETOLD BY

ELLA YOUNG

ILLUSTRATED AND DECORATED BY

MAUD GONNE

DOVER PUBLICATIONS, INC.
New York

Published in Canada by General Publishing Company, Ltd., 30 Lesmill Road, Don Mills, Toronto, Ontario.

Published in the United Kingdom by Constable and Company, Ltd., 3 The Lanchesters, 162–164 Fulham Palace Road, London W6 9ER.

Bibliographical Note

This Dover edition, first published in 1995, is an unabridged republication of the work first published by Maunsel & Company, Dublin, Ireland, 1910. In this edition the four illustrations listed on p. viii, originally in color, have been reprinted in black and white. In addition, a decoration originally appearing on the back of the title page has been moved to the page immediately before that of the frontispiece.

Library of Congress Cataloging-in-Publication Data

Young, Ella, 1867–1956.

Celtic wonder-tales / retold by Ella Young ; illustrated and decorated by Maud Gonne.

p.   cm.

Contents: The earth-shapers—The spear of victory—A good action—How the son of the Gobhaun Saor sold the sheepskin in—How the son of the Gobhaun Saor shortened the road—The cow of plenty—The coming of Luch—The Eric-fine of Luch—The great battle—Inisfail—The golden fly—The children of Lir—The luck-child—Conary Mor.

ISBN 0-486-28896-X (pbk.)

1. Fairy tales—Ireland. [1. Fairy tales. 2. Celts—Folklore. 3. Folklore—Ireland.] I. Gonne, Maud, 1866–1953, ill. II. Title.

PZ8.Y84Ce   1995

398.2'09415—dc20   95-38258
                                                     CIP
                                                     AC

Manufactured in the United States of America
Dover Publications, Inc., 31 East 2nd Street, Mineola, N.Y. 11501

TO

SEAGHAN, ISEULT AND THE PIRATE

AND TO

THE SACRED LAND

CONTENTS

ILLUSTRATIONS

THE   EARTH-SHAPERS

I N Tir-na-Moe, the Land of the Living Heart, Brigit was singing. Angus the Ever-Young, and Midyir the Red-Maned, and Ogma that is called Splendour of the Sun, and the Dagda and other lords of the people of Dana drew near to listen.

Brigit sang:

Now comes the hour foretold, a god-gift bringing
  A wonder-sight.
Is it a star new-born and splendid up springing
  Out of the night?
Is it a wave from the Fountain of Beauty upflinging
  Foam of delight?
Is it a glorious immortal bird that is winging
  Hither its flight?

It is a wave, high-crested, melodious, triumphant,
  Breaking in light.
It is a star, rose-hearted and joyous, a splendour
  Risen from night.
It is flame from the world of the gods, and love
runs before it,
  A quenchless delight.

3

Celtic Wonder-Tales

*Let the wave break, let the star rise, let the flame
leap.
Ours, if our hearts are wise,
To take and keep.*

Brigit ceased to sing, and there was silence
for a little space in Tir-na-Moe. Then Angus
said :

" Strange are the words of your song, and
strange the music : it swept me down steeps of
air—down—down—always further down. Tir-
na-Moe was like a dream half-remembered. I
felt the breath of strange worlds on my face, and
always your song grew louder and louder, but
you were not singing it. Who was singing it ? "

" The Earth was singing it."

" The Earth ! " said the Dagda. " Is not the
Earth in the pit of chaos ? Who has ever looked
into that pit or stayed to listen where there is
neither silence nor song ? "

" O Shepherd of the Star-Flocks, I have stayed
to listen. I have shuddered in the darkness that
is round the Earth. I have seen the black hissing
waters and the monsters that devour each other—
I have looked into the groping writhing adder-pit
of hell."

The light that pulsed about the De Danaan
lords grew troubled at the thought of that pit,
and they cried out : " Tell us no more about
the Earth, O Flame of the Two Eternities, and
let the thought of it slip from yourself as a dream
slips from the memory."

4

The Earth-Shapers

" O Silver Branches that no Sorrow has Shaken,"
said Brigit, " hear one thing more ! The Earth
wails all night because it has dreamed of beauty."

" What dream, O Brigit ? "

" The Earth has dreamed of the white stillness
of dawn ; of the star that goes before the sunrise ;
and of music like the music of my song."

" O Morning Star," said Angus, " would I
had never heard your song, for now I cannot
shake the thought of the Earth from me ! "

" Why should you shake the thought from you,
Angus the Subtle-Hearted ? You have wrapped
yourself in all the colours of the sunlight ; are you
not fain to look into the darkness and listen to
the thunder of abysmal waves ; are you not fain
to make gladness in the Abyss ? "

Angus did not answer : he reached out his
hand and gathered a blossom from a branch :
he blew upon the blossom and tossed it into the
air : it became a wonderful white bird, and circled
about him singing.

Midyir the Haughty rose and shook out the
bright tresses of his hair till he was clothed with
radiance as with a Golden Fleece.

" I am fain to look into the darkness," he said.
" I am fain to hear the thunder of the Abyss."

" Then come with me," said Brigit, " I am
going to put my mantle round the Earth because
it has dreamed of beauty."

" I will make clear a place for your mantle,"
said Midyir. " I will throw fire amongst the
monsters."

5

Celtic Wonder-Tales

"I will go with you too," said the Dagda, who is called the Green Harper.

"And I," said Splendour of the Sun, whose other name is Ogma the Wise. "And I," said Nuada Wielder of the White Light. "And I," said Gobniu the Wonder-Smith, "we will re-make the Earth!"

"Good luck to the adventure!" said Angus. "I would go myself if ye had the Sword of Light with you."

"We will take the Sword of Light," said Brigit, "and the Cauldron of Plenty and the Spear of Victory and the Stone of Destiny with us, for we will build power and wisdom and beauty and lavish-heartedness into the Earth."

"It is well said," cried all the Shining Ones. "We will take the Four Jewels."

Ogma brought the Sword of Light from Findrias the cloud-fair city that is in the east of the De Danaan world; Nuada brought the Spear of Victory from Gorias the flame-bright city that is in the south of the De Danaan world; the Dagda brought the Cauldron of Plenty from Murias the city that is builded in the west of the De Danaan world and has the stillness of deep waters; Midyir brought the Stone of Destiny from Falias the city that is builded in the north of the De Danaan world and has the steadfastness of adamant. Then Brigit and her companions set forth.

They fell like a rain of stars till they came to the blackness that surrounded the Earth, and

The Earth-Shapers

looking down saw below them, as at the bottom
of an abyss, the writhing, contorted, hideous
life that swarmed and groped and devoured
itself ceaselessly.

From the seething turmoil of that abyss all
the Shining Ones drew back save Midyir.   He
grasped the Fiery Spear and descended like a
flame.

His comrades looked down and saw him treading
out the monstrous life as men tread grapes in
a wine-press ; they saw the blood and foam of
that destruction rise about Midyir till he was
crimson with it even to the crown of his head ;
they saw him whirl the Spear till it became a
wheel of fire and shot out sparks and tongues of
flame ; they saw the flame lick the darkness and
turn back on itself and spread and blossom—
murk-red—blood-red—rose-red at last !

Midyir drew himself out of the abyss, a Ruby
Splendour, and said :

" I have made a place for Brigit's mantle.
Throw down your mantle, Brigit, and bless the
Earth ! "

Brigit threw down her mantle and when it
touched the Earth it spread itself, unrolling like
silver flame.   It took possession of the place
Midyir had made as the sea takes possession, and
it continued to spread itself because everything
that was foul drew back from the little silver
flame at the edge of it.

It is likely it would have spread itself over all
the earth, only Angus, the youngest of the gods,

7

had not patience to wait : he leaped down and stood with his two feet on the mantle. It ceased to be fire and became a silver mist about him. He ran through the mist laughing and calling on the others to follow. His laughter drew them and they followed. The drifting silver mist closed over them and round them, and through it they saw each other like images in a dream—changed and fantastic. They laughed when they saw each other. The Dagda thrust both his hands into the Cauldron of Plenty.

" O Cauldron," he said, " you give to every one the gift that is meetest, give me now a gift meet for the Earth."

He drew forth his hands full of green fire and he scattered the greenness everywhere as a sower scatters seed. Angus stooped and lifted the greenness of the earth ; he scooped hollows in it ; he piled it in heaps ; he played with it as a child plays with sand, and when it slipped through his fingers it changed colour and shone like star-dust— blue and purple and yellow and white and red.

Now, while the Dagda sowed emerald fire and Angus played with it, Mananaun was aware that the exiled monstrous life had lifted itself and was looking over the edge of Brigit's mantle. He saw the iron eyes of strange creatures jeering in the blackness and he drew the Sword of Light from its scabbard and advanced its gleaming edge against that chaos. The strange life fled in hissing spume, but the sea rose to greet the Sword in a great foaming thunderous wave.

The Earth-Shapers

Mananaun swung the Sword a second time, and the sea rose again in a wave that was green as a crysolite, murmurous, sweet-sounding, flecked at the edges with amythest and purple and blue-white foam.

A third time Mananaun swung the Sword, and the sea rose to greet it in a wave white as crystal, unbroken, continuous, silent as dawn.

The slow wave fell back into the sea, and Brigit lifted her mantle like a silver mist. The De Danaans saw everything clearly. They saw that they were in an island covered with green grass and full of heights and strange scooped-out hollows and winding ways. They saw too that the grass was full of flowers—blue and purple and yellow and white and red.

" Let us stay here," they said to each other, " and make beautiful things so that the Earth may be glad."

Brigit took the Stone of Destiny in her hands : it shone white like a crystal between her hands.

" I will lay the Stone in this place," she said, " that ye may have empire."

She laid the Stone on the green grass and it sank into the earth : a music rose about it as it sank, and suddenly all the scooped-out hollows and deep winding ways were filled with water— rivers of water that leaped and shone ; lakes and deep pools of water trembling into stillness.

" It is the laughter of the Earth ! " said Ogma the Wise.

Angus dipped his fingers in the water.

"I would like to see the blue and silver fishes that swim in Connla's Well swimming here," he said, "and trees growing in this land like those trees with blossomed branches that grow in the Land of the Silver Fleece."

"It is an idle wish, Angus the Young," said Ogma. "The fishes in Connla's Well are too bright for these waters and the blossoms that grow on silver branches would wither here. We must wait and learn the secret of the Earth, and slowly fashion dark strange trees, and fishes that are not like the fishes in Connla's Well."

"Yea," said Nuada, "we will fashion other trees, and under their branches shall go hounds that are not like the hound Failinis and deer that have not horns of gold. We will make ourselves the smiths and artificers of the world and beat the strange life out yonder into other shapes. We will make for ourselves islands to the north of this and islands to the west, and round them shall go also the three waves of Mananaun for we will fashion and re-fashion all things till there is nothing unbeautiful left in the whole earth."

"It is good work," cried all the De Danaans, "we will stay and do it, but Brigit must go to Moy Mell and Tir-na-Moe and Tir-nan-Oge and Tir-fo-Tonn, and all the other worlds, for she is the Flame of Delight in every one of them."

"Yes, I must go," said Brigit.

"O Brigit!" said Ogma, "before you go, tie a knot of remembrance in the fringe of your mantle so that you may always remember this

The Earth-Shapers

place—and tell us, too, by what name we shall call this place."

" Ye shall call it the White Island," said Brigit, " and its other name shall be the Island of Destiny ; and its other name shall be Ireland."

Then Ogma tied a knot of remembrance in the fringe of Brigit's mantle.

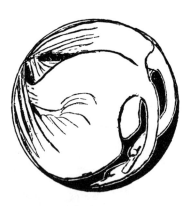

THE SPEAR OF VICTORY

UADA, Wielder of the White Light, set up the Spear of Victory in the centre of Ireland. It was like a great fiery fountain. It was like a singing flame. It burned continually, and from it every fire in Ireland was kindled. The glow of it reached up to the mountain tops. The glow of it reached under the forest trees. The glow of it shot into the darkness and made a halo of light far beyond the three waves of Mananaun. The mis-shapen things of the darkness came to the edge of the halo. They sunned themselves in it They got strength from it. They began to build a habitation for themselves in the dark waters. They took shapes to themselves, and dark cunning

15

wisdom. Balor the One-Eyed was their king. They were minded to get the Spear of Victory.

They compassed Ireland. They made a harsh screeching. The De Danaans said to each other:

"It is only the Fomor, the people from under the sea, who are screeching; they will tire of it!"

They did not tire of it: they kept up the screeching. The De Danaans tired of it. Nuada took up the Spear of Victory. He whirled it. He threw it into the blackness that it might destroy the Fomor. It went through them like lightning through storm-clouds. It made a great destruction. Balor grasped it. He had the grip! The Spear stayed with him. It was like a fiery serpent twisting every way. He brought it into his own country. There was a lake in the middle of his own country full of black water. Whoever tasted that water would forget anything he knew. Balor put the fiery head of the Spear in that lake. It became a column of red-hot iron. He could not draw it out of the lake.

The Spear was in the lake then. Great clouds of steam rose about it from the black water. Out of the hissing steam Demons of the Air were born. The Demons were great and terrible. There was an icy wind about them. They found their way into Ireland. They took prey there in spite of the De Danaans. They made broad tracks for themselves. The Fomor followed in their tracks. It was then that misfortune came to the De Danaans. The people of the Fomor got

The Spear of Victory

the better of the De Danaans. They took the Cauldron of Plenty and the Magic Harp from the Dagda. They made themselves lords and hard rulers over the De Danaans, and they laid Ireland under tribute. They were taking tribute out of it ever and again till Lugh Lauve Fauda came. 'Twas he that broke the power of the Fomor and sent the three sons of Dana for the Spear. They had power to draw it out of the lake. They gave it to Lugh, and it is with him it is now, and 'tis he will set it up again in the middle of Ireland before the end of the world.

A GOOD ACTION

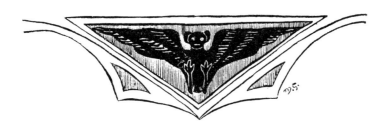

HE DAGDA sat with his back to an oak tree. He looked like a workman, and his hands were as hard as the hands of a mason, but his hair was braided like the hair of a king. He had on a green cloak with nine capes, and along the border of every cape there was a running pattern embroidered in gold and silver and purple thread. Opposite the Dagda sat his son, Angus Og, with his hands clasped about his knees. He was in rags, and his hair was matted like the hair of a beggar: a bramble had scratched his nose, but his eyes were smiling.

"If you only knew how ridiculous you look in that cloak," he was saying to the Dagda, "you would not wear it."

"My son," said the Dagda, with dignity, "it is the only cloak the people of the Fomor have left me, and the evening is cold."

"Why don't you keep yourself warm by working?" said Angus. "It's what I would do myself if you had brought me up to a trade."

"Angus," said his father, "remember I am one of the gods: it is not necessary to talk sense to me."

"O dear!" said Angus, "a bramble scratched me on the nose this morning—it's all because you have lost your Magic Harp and the Cauldron of Plenty! Soon even the snails will make faces at me. I can't go wandering round Ireland in comfort any more. I'll change myself into a salmon and swim in the sea."

"The salmon must come up the rivers once a year, and when you come the Fomorians will take you in their net, and it is likely Balor, their king, will eat you."

"'Ochone a rie!' I must be something else! I'll be an eagle."

"You will shiver in the icy grip of the wind that goes before the Fomor—the black bitter wind that blows them hither to darken the sun for us."

"'Ochone, Ochone, my Grief and my Trouble!' I must think of something else. I'll be a good action. The Fomor never meddle with a good action."

While Angus was talking a Pooka came out from between the trees. It looked like a little snow-white kid with golden horns and silver hoofs, but it could take any shape it had a fancy for. When it saw Angus it smiled and made one jump on to his shoulder.

"Look at this!" said Angus. "I never can say anything important without being interrupted!"

A Good Action

"What do you want ? " he said to the Pooka, pretending to be cross.

"O nothing at all, only to listen to your wise talk ; it does me good," said the Pooka, prancing on Angus' shoulder.

"Well, keep quiet if you want to listen ! " said Angus. "I was saying," he continued to the Dagda, "I will be a good action."

Just at that moment an ugly deformed animal, with a head like the head of a pig and a hound's body, came tearing through the wood ; behind it was a young boy of the Fomor. He was ugly and deformed, but he had a rich cloak and a gold circle on his head. The moment he saw the Pooka he threw a fire-ball at it. The Pooka jumped behind Angus, and Angus caught the fire-ball. It went out in his hand.

"I am a Prince of the Fomor," said the boy, trying to look big.

"I was thinking as much," said Angus ; "you have princely manners."

"I am Balor's own son. I have come out to look for treasure, and if you have anything I command you to give it to me at once."

"What would you like ? " said Angus.

"I would like the white horse of Mananaun ; or three golden apples ; or a hound out of Tir-nan-Oge."

"They say it's lucky to be good to poor folk," said Angus. "If you are good to us, perhaps you may find a treasure."

"If you do not get up at once and hunt about

Celtic Wonder-Tales

for a treasure for me I will tell my father, Balor, and he will wither you off the face of the earth ! "

" O give me a little time," said Angus, " and I'll look for something."

The Pooka, who had been listening to everything, now skipped out from his hiding-place with a turnip in his mouth—he was holding it by the green leaves.

" The very thing ! " said Angus. " Here is a treasure ! " He took the turnip in his hands and passed his fingers over it. The turnip became a great white egg, and the leaves turned into gold and crimson spots and spread themselves over the egg.

" Now, look at this ! " said Angus. " It is an enchanted egg. You have only to keep it till you do three Good Actions, and then it will hatch out into something splendid."

" Will it hatch into Mananaun's white horse ? " said the boy.

" It depends on the Good Actions you do ; everything depends on that."

" What is a Good Action ? "

" Well, if you were to go quietly away, and never tell any one you had seen us, it would be a Good Action."

" I'll go," said the boy. He took the egg in his hands, kicked up a toe-full of earth at the Pooka, and went.

He hadn't gone far when he heard a bird singing. He looked and saw a little bird on a furze-bush.

24

A Good Action

" Stop that noise ! " he said.

The bird went on singing. The boy flung the egg at it. The egg turned into a turnip and struck a hare. The hare jumped out of the furze-bush.

" My curse on you," said the boy, " for a brittle egg ! What came over you to hatch into nothing better than a hare ! My Grief and my Trouble ! what came over you to hatch out at all when this is only my second Good Action ? "

He set his hound after the hare, but the hare had touched the enchanted turnip and got some of the magic, so the hound could not chase it. He came back with the turnip. The boy hit him over the head with it many times and the dog howled. His howling soothed Balor's son, and after a while he left off beating the dog and turned to go back to his own country. At first he walked with big steps puffing his cheeks vaingloriously, but little by little a sense of loss overcame him, and as he thought how nearly he had earned the white horse of Mananaun, or three golden apples, or some greater treasure, two tears slowly rolled down his snub nose : they were the first tears he had shed in his life.

Angus and the Dagda and the Pooka were still in the little clearing when Balor's son passed back through it. The moment he came in sight the Pooka changed himself into a squirrel and ran up the oak tree ; Angus changed himself into a turnip and lay at the Dagda's feet ; but the Dagda, who had not time to think of a suitable transformation, sat quite still and looked at the young Fomorian.

"Sshh! Sshh! Hii! Tear him, dog!" said Balor's son.

The pig-headed creature rushed at the Dagda, but when he came to the turnip he ran back howling. The Dagda smiled and picked up the turnip. He pressed his hands over it and it became a great golden egg with green and purple spots on it.

"Give it to me! Give it to me!" yelled Balor's son, "it's better than the first egg, and the first egg is broken. Give it to me."

"This egg is too precious for you," said the Dagda. "I must keep it in my own hands."

"Then I will blast you and all the forest and every living thing! I have only to roar three times, and three armies of my people will come to help me. Give me the egg or I will roar."

"I will keep this egg in my own hands," said the Dagda.

Balor's son shut his eyes tight and opened his mouth very wide to let out a great roar, and it is likely he would have been heard at the other end of the world if the Pooka hadn't dropped a handful of acorns into his mouth. The roar never came out. Balor's son choked and spluttered, and the Dagda patted him on the back and shook him. He shook him very hard, and while he shook him Angus turned into a good action and slipped into the boy's mind. Balor's son got his breath then, he said:

A Good Action

"I will not blast you this time; I will do a Good Action. I will let you carry the egg, and you can be my slave and treasure-finder."

"Thank you," said the Dagda; but the words were scarcely out of his mouth when a terrible icy wind swept through the wood. The earth shook and the trees bent and twisted with terror. The Pooka instantly turned himself into a dead leaf and dropped into a fold of the Dagda's cloak; the Dagda hid the leaf in his bosom and turned his cloak so that the nine capes were inside. He did it all in a moment, and the next moment the wood was full of Fomorians—ugly mis-shapen beings with twisted mouths and squinting eyes. They shouted with joy when they saw Balor's son, but they knew the Dagda was one of the De Danaans and rushed at him with their weapons.

"Stop!" roared Balor's son. "Keep back from my Treasure-Finder! He must follow me wherever I go."

The Fomor stood back from the Dagda, and their captain bowed himself before Balor's son.

"O Prince," he said, "whose mouth drops honey and wisdom, the thing shall be as you command, and, O Light of our Countenance, come with us now, for the Harp-feast is beginning and Balor has sent us into the four quarters of the world to find you."

"What feast are you talking about?"

"O Pearl of Goodness, the feast your father is giving so that all his lords may see the great harp that was taken from the Dagda."

"I know all about that harp! I have seen it; no one can play on it—I will not go with you!"

"O Fount of Generosity, we are all as good as dead if we return without you."

Balor's son turned away and took two steps into the wood; then he stopped and balanced himself, first on one foot then on the other; then he turned round and gave a great sigh.

"I will go with you," he said, "it is my twenty-first Good Action!"

The terrible icy wind swept through the wood again and the Fomorians rose into it as dust rises in a whirlwind; the Dagda rose too, and the wind swept the whole company into Balor's country.

It was a country as hard as iron with never a flower or a blade of grass to be seen and a sky over it where the sun and moon never showed themselves. The place of feasting was a great plain and the hosts of the Fomor were gathered thick upon it. Balor of the Evil Eye was in the midst and beside him the great harp. Every string of the harp shone with the colours of the rainbow and a golden flame moved about it. No one of the Fomor had power to play on it.

As soon as the Dagda saw the harp he turned his cloak in the twinkling of an eye so that the nine capes were outmost and he stretched his hands and cried:

> "Taip Daup-dablao,
> Taip Coip cethapchuin,
> Taip pam, taip gam,
> Deola cpoc ocup bolg ocup buinne."

28

A Good Action

The great harp gave a leap to him. It went through the hosts of the Fomor like lightning through clouds, and they perished before it like stubble before flame. The Dagda struck one note on it, and all the Fomor lost the power to move or speak. Then he began to play, and through that iron country grass and flowers came up, slender apple-trees grew and blossomed, and over them the sky was blue without a cloud. The Pooka turned himself into a spotted fawn and danced between the trees. Angus drew himself out of the mind of Balor's son and stood beside the Dagda. He did not look like a beggar-man. He had a golden light round his head and a purple cloak like a purple cloud, and all about him circled beautiful white birds. The wind from the birds' wings blew the blossoms from the apple trees and the petals drifted with sleepy magic into the minds of the Fomorians, so that each one bowed his head and slept. When the Dagda saw that, he changed the tune he was playing, and the grass and flowers became a dust of stars and vanished. The apple trees vanished one by one till there was only one left. It was covered over with big yellow apples—sweeter than the sweetest apples any one ever ate. It moved, and Angus saw it was going to vanish. He put his hand on the Dagda's wrist to stop the music and said:

"Do not play away that apple tree. Leave it for Balor's son when he wakens—after all, he did one Good Action."

The Dagda smiled and stopped playing.

HOW THE SON
OF THE GOBHAUN SAOR
SOLD THE SHEEPSKIN

THE GOBHAUN SAOR was a great person in the old days, and he looked to his son to be a credit to him. He had only one son, and thought the world and all of him, but that was nothing to what the son thought of himself. He was growing up every day, and the more he grew up the more he thought of himself, till at last the Gobhaun Saor's house was too small to hold him, and the Gobhaun said it was time for him to go out and seek his fortune. He gave him a sheepskin and his blessing, and said:

"Take this sheepskin and go into the fair and let me see what cleverness you have in selling it."

"I'll do that," said the son, "and bring you the best price to be got in the fair."

"That's little," said the Gobhaun Saor, "but if you were to bring me the skin and the price of it, I'd say you had cleverness."

"Then that's what I'll bring you!" said the son, and he set off on his travels.

"What do you want for that sheepskin you have?" said the first man he met in the fair. He named his price.

"'Tis a good price," said the man, "but the skin is good, and I have no time for bargaining; here is the money; give me the skin."

"I can't agree to that," said the son of the Gobhaun Saor. "I must have the skin and the price of it too."

"I hope you may get it!" said the man, and he went away laughing. That was the way with all the men that tried to buy the skin, and at last the son of the Gobhaun Saor was tired of trying to sell it, and when he saw a crowd of people standing around a beggar man he went and stood with the rest. The beggar man was doing tricks and every one was watching him. After a while he called out:

"Lend me that sheepskin of yours and I'll show you a trick with it!"

"You needn't ask for the loan of that skin," said one of the men standing by, "for the owner of it wants to keep it and sell it at the same time, there's so much cleverness in him!"

The son of the Gobhaun Saor was angry when that was said, and he flung down the skin to the juggler-man.

"Do a trick with it if you can," said he.

The beggar man spread out the skin and blew between the wool of it, and a great wood sprang

The Sheepskin

up—miles and miles of a dark wood—and there were trees in it with golden apples. The people were frightened when they saw it, but the beggar man walked into the wood till the trees hid him. There was sorrow on the son of the Gobhaun Saor at that.

"Now I'll never give my father either the skin or the price of it," he said to himself, "but the least I may do is to take him an apple off the trees." He put out his hand to an apple, and when he touched it he had only a bit of wool in his hand. The sheepskin was before him. He took it up and went out of the fair.

He was walking along the roads then and it was growing dark and he was feeling sorry for himself, when he saw the light of a house. He went toward it, and when he came to it the door was open, and in the little room inside he saw the beggar man of the fair and another man stirring a big pot.

"Come in," said the beggar man; "this is the house of the Dagda Mor, the World Builder. It isn't much, as you see, but you may rest here and welcome, and maybe the Dagda will give us supper."

"Son Angus," said the Dagda to the beggar man, "you talk as if I had the Cauldron of Plenty, and you know well that it is gone from me. The Fomorians have it now and I have only this pot. Hard enough it is to fill it, and when it is filled I never get a good meal out of it, for a great, hulking, splay-footed churl of a Fomorian comes in when he smells the meat and takes all the best of it from me, and I have only what remains when he has gorged himself; so I am always hungry, son Angus."

"Your case is hard," said Angus, "but I know how you can help yourself."

"Tell me how," said the Dagda.

"Well," said Angus, "get a piece of gold and put it into the best part of the meat, and when the Fomorian has eaten it up tell him he has swallowed the gold; his heart will burst when he hears that, and you'll be rid of him."

"Your plan is good," said the Dagda, "but where am I to get the gold? The Fomorians keep me building all day for them, but they give me nothing."

"I wish I had a piece of gold to give you myself," said Angus. "'Tis a bad thing to be a beggar man! The next time I disguise myself I'll be a prince." He laughed at that, but the Dagda stirred the pot and looked gloomy. The son of the Gobhaun Saor felt sorry for him and remembered that he had a gold ring his father had given him. He pulled it off his finger and gave it to the Dagda.

"Here," said he, "is a piece of gold and you can be rid of the Fomorian."

The Dagda thanked him and gave him his blessing and they spent the night in peace and happiness till morning reddened the sky.

When the son of the Gobhaun Saor started to go, Angus set him a bit on the way.

The Sheepskin

"You are free-handed," he said to him, "and a credit to your father, and now I'll give you a bit of advice—Say 'Good morrow kindly' to the first woman you can meet on the road, and good luck be with you."

It wasn't long till the son of the Gobhaun Saor saw a woman at a little stream washing clothes. "Good luck to the work," he said, "and good morrow kindly."

"Good morrow to yourself," said she, "and may your load be light."

"It would need to be light," said he, "for I'll have far enough to carry it."

"Why so?" said she.

"I must carry it till I meet some one to give me the price of it and the skin as well."

"You need travel no further for that," said she; "give me the sheepskin."

"With a heart and a half," said he, and he gave her the skin. She paid the price, and she plucked the wool from the skin and threw him the skin.

"Now you can go home to your father," she said.

He wasn't long going, and he was proud when he gave the Gobhaun the skin and the price of it.

"What man showed you the wise way out of it?" said the Gobhaun Saor.

"No man at all," said the son, "but a woman."

"And you met a woman like that, and hadn't the wit to bring her with you!" said the Gobhaun Saor. "Away with you now, and don't let the wind that is behind you come up with you till you ask her to marry you!"

Celtic Wonder-Tales

The son didn't need the second word, and the wind didn't overtake him till he asked the woman to marry him. They came back together, and the Gobhaun made a wedding feast for them that was remembered year in and year out for a hundred years.

HOW THE SON OF THE GOBHAUN SAOR SHORTENED THE ROAD

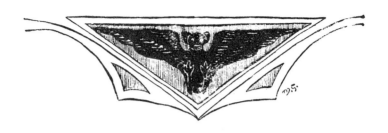

NE day the Son of the Gobhaun Saor was sitting outside in the sunshine, cutting a little reed into a pipe to make music with. He was so busy that he never saw three stranger-men coming till they were close to him. He looked up then and saw three thrawn-faced churls wrapped in long cloaks. "Good morrow to you," said the Son of the Gobhaun Saor. "Good morrow," said they. "We have come to say a word to the Son of the Gobhaun Saor." "He is before you," said the Son. "We have come," said the most thrawn-faced of the three, "from the King of the Land Under Wave to ask you to help him; he has a piece of work that none of his own people can do, and you have the cleverness of the Three Worlds in your fingers." "'Tis my father has that," said the Son of the Gobhaun Saor. "Well," said the other, "bring your father with you to the Land Under Wave and your fortune's made."

The Son of the Gobhaun Saor set off at that to find his father. "I have the news of the world for you and your share of fortune out of it," he said. "What news?" said the Gobhaun. "The King of the Land Under Wave has sent for me; if you come with me your fortune is made." "Did he send you a token?" "No token at all, but do you think I would not know his messengers?" "O, 'tis you has the cleverness!" said the Gobhaun Saor.

They set out next morning, and as they were going along, the Gobhaun Saor said: "Son, shorten the way for me." "How could I do that?" said the Son, "if your own two feet can't shorten it." "Now, do you think," said the father, "that you'll make my fortune and your own too when you can't do a little thing like that!" and he went back to the house.

The Son sat down on a stone with his head on his hands to think how he could shorten the road, but the more he thought of it the harder it seemed, and after a while he gave up thinking and began to look round him. He saw a wide stretch of green grass and an old man spreading out locks of wool on it. The old man was frail and bent, and he moved slowly spreading out the wool. The Son of the Gobhaun Saor thought it hard to see the old man working, and went to help him, but when he came nearer a little wind caught the wool and it lifted and drifted, and he saw it wasn't wool at all but white foam of the sea. The old man straightened himself, and the Son of the Gobhaun Saor knew it was Mananaun the Sea-God, and he stood

The Shortening of the Road

with his eyes on the sea-foam and had nothing to say. "You came to help me," said Mananaun. "I did," said the Son of the Gobhaun Saor, "but you need no help from me." "The outstretched hand," said Mananaun, "is the hand that is filled the fullest; stoop now and take a lock of my wool, it will help you when you need help." The Son of the Gobhaun Saor stooped to the sea-foam; the wind was blowing it, and under the foam he saw the blue of the sea clear as crystal, and under that a field of red flowers bending with the wind. He took a handful of foam. It became a lock of wool, and when he raised himself Mananaun was gone, and there was nothing before him but the greenness of grass and the sun shining on it.

He went home then and showed the lock of wool to his wife and told her the sorrow he was in because he couldn't shorten the road for his father. "Don't be in sorrow for that," said she, "sure every one knows that story-telling is the way to shorten a road." "May wisdom grow with you like the tree that has the nuts of knowledge!" said he. "I'll take your advice, and maybe to-morrow my father won't turn back on the road."

They set out next day and the Gobhaun Saor said—"Son, be shortening the road." At that the Son began the story of Angus Oge and how he won a house for himself from the Dagda Mor: it was a long story, and he made it last till they came to the White Strand.

When they got there they saw a clumsy ill-made boat waiting for them, with ugly dark-looking men to row it.

" Since when," said the Gobhaun Saor, " did the King of the Land Under Wave get Fomorians to be his rowers, and when did he borrow a boat from them ? " The Son had no word to answer him, but the ugliest of the ill-made lot came up to them with two cloaks in his hand that shone like the sea when the Sun strikes lights out of it. " These cloaks," said he, " are from the Land Under Wave ; put one about your head, Gobhaun Saor, and you won't think the boat ugly or the journey long." " What did I tell you ? " said the Son when he saw the cloaks. " You have your own asking of a token, and if you turn back now in spite of the way I shortened the road for you, I'll go myself and I'll have luck with me." " I'll go with you," said the Gobhaun Saor ; he took the cloaks and they stepped into the boat. He put one round his head the way he wouldn't see the ugly oarsmen, and the Son took the other.

As they were coming near land the Gobhaun Saor looked out from the cloak, and when he saw the place he pulled the cloak from his Son's head and said : " Look at the land we are coming to." It was a dark, dreary, death-looking country without grass or trees or sun in the sky. " I'm thinking it won't take long to spend the fortune you'll make here," said the Gobhaun Saor, " for this is not the Land Under Wave but the country of Balor of the Evil Eye, the King of the

The Shortening of the Road

Fomorians." He stood up then and called to the chief of the oarsmen: "You trapped us with lies and with cloaks stolen from the Land Under Wave, but you'll trap no one else with the cloaks," and he flung them into the sea. They sank at once as if hands pulled them down. "Let them go back to their owners," said the Gobhaun Saor.

The Fomorians ground their teeth and cursed with rage, but they were afraid to touch the Gobhaun or his Son because Balor wanted them; so they guarded them carefully and brought them to the King. He was a big mis-shapen giant with a terrible eye that blasted everything, and he lived in a great dun made of glass as smooth and cold as ice. "You are a fire-smith and a wonder-smith, and your Son is a wise man," he said to the Gobhaun. "I have brought the two of you here to put fire under a pot for me." "That is no hard task," said the Gobhaun. "Show me the pot." "I will," said Balor, and he brought them to a walled-in place that was guarded all round by warriors. Inside was the largest pot the Gobhaun Saor had ever laid eyes on; it was made of red bronze riveted together, and it shone like the Sun. "I want you to light a fire under that pot," said Balor." "None of my own people can light a fire under it, and every fire over which it is hung goes out. Your choice of good fortune to you if you put fire under the pot, and clouds of misfortune to you if you fail, for then neither yourself nor your Son will leave the place alive."

"Let every one go out of the enclosure but my Son and myself," said the Gobhaun Saor, "until we see what power we have." They went out, and when the Gobhaun Saor got the place to himself he said to the Son: "Go round the pot from East to West, and I will go round from West to East, and see what wisdom comes to us." They went round nine times, and then the Gobhaun Saor said: "Son, what wisdom came to you?" "I think," said the Son, "this pot belongs to the Dagda Mor." "There is truth on your tongue," said the Gobhaun, "for it is the Cauldron of Plenty that used to feed all the men of Ireland at one time, when the Dagda had it, and every one got out of it the food he liked best. It was by stealth and treachery the Fomorians got it, and that is why they cannot put fire under it." With that he let a shout to the Fomorians: "Come in now, for I have wisdom on me." "Are you going to light the fire," said the Son, "for the robbers that have destroyed Ireland?" "Whist," said the Gobhaun Saor; "who said I was going to light the fire?" "Tell Balor," he said to the Fomorians that came running in, "that I must have nine kinds of wood freshly gathered to put under the pot and two stones to strike fire from. Get me boughs of the oak, boughs of the ash, boughs of the pine tree, boughs of the quicken, boughs of the blackthorn, boughs of the hazel, boughs of the yew, boughs of the whitethorn, and a branch of bog myrtle; and bring me a

The Shortening of the Road

white stone from the door step of a Brugh-fer, and a black stone from the door step of a poet that has the nine golden songs, and I will put fire under the pot."

They ran to Balor with the news, and he grew black with rage when he heard it. "Where am I to get boughs of the oak, boughs of the ash, boughs of the pine tree, boughs of the quicken, boughs of the blackthorn, boughs of the hazel, boughs of the yew, boughs of the white-thorn and a branch of bog myrtle in a country as barren as the grave?" said he. "What poet of mine knows any songs that are not satires or maledictions, and what Brugh-fer have I who never gave a meal's meat to a stranger all my life? Let him tell us," said Balor, "how the things are to be got?" They went back to the Gobhaun Saor then and asked how the things were to be got. "It is hard," said the Gobhaun, "to do anything in a country like this, but since you have none of the things, you must go to the Land of the De Danaans for them. Let Balor's Son and his Sister's Son go to my house in Ireland and ask the woman of the house for the things."

Balor's Son set out and the Son of Balor's Sister with him. Balor's Druids sent a wind behind them that swept them into the country of the De Danaans like a blast of winter. They came to the house of the Gobhaun Saor, and the wife of the Son came out to them. "O Woman of the House," said they, "we have a message from the Gobhaun Saor." He is to light a fire

47

for Balor, and he sent us to ask you for boughs
of the oak, boughs of the ash, boughs of the pine
tree, boughs of the quicken, boughs of the blackthorn, boughs of the hazel, boughs of the yew,
boughs of the whitethorn and a branch of bog
myrtle. "You are to give us," he said, "a white
stone from the door step of a Brugh-fer, and a
black stone from the door step of a poet that
has the nine golden songs."

"A good asking," said the woman, "and
welcome before you!" "Let the Son of Balor
come into the secret chamber of the house." He
came in, and she said: "Show me the token my
man gave you." Now, Balor's Son had no token,
but he wouldn't own to that, so he brought out
a ring and said: "Here is the token." The
woman took it in her hand, and when she touched
it she knew that it belonged to Balor's Son, and
she went out of the room from him and locked
the door on him with seven locks that no one
could open but herself.

She went to the other Fomorian then and
said: "Go to Balor and tell him I have his
Son, and he will not get him back till I get
back the two that went from me, and if he wants
the things you ask for he must send a token from
my own people before I give them."

Balor was neither to hold nor to bind when
he got this news. "Man for man," he said;
"she kept one and she'll get back one, but I'll
have my will of the other. The Gobhaun Saor
will pay dear for sending my Son on a fool's

The Shortening of the Road

errand." He called to his warriors and said: " Shut the Gobhaun Saor and his Son in my strongest dun and guard it well through the night. To-morrow I'll send the Son to Ireland and get back my own Son, and to-morrow I'll have the blood of the Gobhaun Saor."

The Gobhaun Saor and his Son were left in the dun without light, without food, and without companions. Outside they could hear the heavy-footed Fomorians, and the night seemed long to them. " My sorrow," said the Son, " that ever I brought you here to seek a fortune, but put a good thought on me now, father, for we have come to the end of it all." " I needn't blame your wit," said the father, " that had as little myself. Why did I send only two messengers ? Why didn't I send a lucky number like three ? Then she could have kept two and send one back. Troth, from this out every fool will know there's luck in odd numbers ! "

" If we had light itself," said the Son, " it wouldn't be so hard, or if I had a little pipe to play a tune on." He thought of the little reed pipe he was making the day the three Fomorians came to him, and he began to search in the folds of his belt for it. His hand came on the lock of wool he got from Mananaun, and he drew it out. " O the fool that I was," he said, " not to think of this sooner ! " " What have you there ? " said the Gobhaun. " I have a lock of wool from the Sea-God, and it will help me now when I need help." He drew it through his fingers

49

and said : " Give me light !" and all the dun was
full of light. He divided the wool into two
parts and said : " Be cloaks of darkness and
invisibility!" and he had two cloaks in his hand
coloured like the sea where the shadow is deepest.
" Put one about you," he said to the Gobhaun,
and he drew the other round himself. They
went to the door, it flew open before them, a
sleep of enchantment came on the guards and
they went out free. " Now," said the Son of
the Gobhaun Saor, " let a small light go
before us ; and a small light went before
them on the road, for there were no stars in
Balor's sky. When they came to the Dark
Strand the Son struck the waters with his cloak
and a boat came to him. It had neither oars nor
sails ; it was pure crystal, and it was shining
like the big white star that is in the sky before
sunrise. " It is the Ocean-Sweeper," said the
Gobhaun. " Mananaun has sent us his own
boat ! " " My thousand welcomes before it,"
said the Son, " and good fortune and honour
to Mananaun while there is one wave to run
after another in the sea ! "

They stepped into the boat, and no sooner had
they stepped into it than they were at the White
Strand, for the Ocean-Sweeper goes as fast as
a thought goes, and takes the people she carries
at once to the place they have their hearts on.
" It is a good sight our own land is ! " said the
Gobhaun when his feet touched Ireland. " It
is," said the Son, " and may we live long to

The Shortening of the Road

see it!" There was no stopping after that till they reached the house of the Gobhaun, and right glad was the Woman of the House to see them. They told her all their story, and she told them how she had seven locks on Balor's Son. "Let him out now," said the Gobhaun, "and ask the men of Ireland to a feast and let the Fomorian take back a good account of the treatment he got."

Well, there was the feast of the world that night. The biggest pot in the Gobhaun's house was hung up, and the Gobhaun himself put fire under it. He took boughs of the oak, boughs of the ash, boughs of the pine tree, boughs of the quicken, boughs of the blackthorn, boughs of the hazel, boughs of the yew, boughs of the whitethorn, and a branch of bog-myrtle. He got a white stone from the door-step of a Brugh-fer, and a black stone from the door-step of a poet that had nine golden songs. He struck fire from the stones and the flames leaped up under the pot, red blue and scarlet and every colour of the rainbow.

It is not dark or silent Gobhaun's house was that night, and if all the champions on the golden crested ridge of the world had come into it with the hunger of seven years on them they could have lost it without trouble at Gobhaun's feast.

THE COW OF PLENTY

OBNIU, the Smith, had the Cow of Plenty. She walked all over Ireland in a day's grazing and gave milk to every one that came to her: there was no one hungry or sorrowful in Ireland in those days!

Balor of the Evil Eye set his heart on the Cow. He had the grasping hand that is never filled, and there was nothing good in his country. He sent the best man he had to steal the Cow of Plenty.

The man stole her, but as he was taking her away Gobniu saw him and let out a battle-roar that shook stars from the sky. The man made a leap into the darkness and got off. Gobniu had the Cow, but the Fomorian had the halter. Now, the luck of the world was in the halter, and wherever the halter was the Cow would follow it. Gobniu got little good of the Cow after that! He had to keep his eyes on her, morning, noon, and night, for fear she would go into Balor's country. He had to tramp behind her when she took her day's grazing all over Ireland, and the days seemed long to Gobniu the Wonder-Smith.

One day a young champion in a red cloak fringed with gold came to him and stood outside his door and saluted him:

"O Wonder-Smith, O Gobniu! will you make a sword for me? It must be long, and keen-edged, and a death-biter—a sword for a champion. Will you make it, Gobniu? No Smith in Ireland can make a sword for champion-feats but yourself!"

"It's little trouble I would have with the sword, young champion, but I must follow my Cow from morning till night. If once I took my eyes off her, she would go to Balor in the land of the Fomor."

"If you make the sword for me I will follow the Cow from morning till night and never take my eyes off her once."

"If you do that, Cian, son of Dian-Cecht, I will make the sword."

It was agreed between them, and the Smith set to the making of the sword while Cian followed the Cow. She walked all over Ireland that day, and Cian was not sorry when she came at night to the house of Gobniu. There was light within, and some men stood at the door. They said to Cian:

"The Wonder-Smith has made the sword for you, and waits to put the tempering on it: he can't do that till you go within and hold the sword hilt."

The Cow of Plenty

It was a joy to Cian to hear this, and he ran in quickly.

"Where is the Cow?" said the Smith.

"She is without," said Cian; "my head to you if she is not!"

"She is not without," said the Smith, "she is with Balor!" and he ran to the door. The Cow was gone!

"I have only my head to give you now, O Gobniu!"

"I will not take your head, Cian, son of Dian-Cecht, but I will take another eric from you. Go now in search of the halter; it is with Balor in the land of the Fomorians. The road is hard to find that leads there and the dark waters are ill to cross, but do not turn back or leave off seeking till you get the halter of the Cow."

"I will not come back to Ireland," said Cian, "without the halter of the Cow."

Cian set out and he travelled and travelled till he came to the dark waters, and when he came to them he could find no boat to cross. He waited there for three days and nights searching for a boat, and then he saw a small poor-looking boat with an old man in it. Cian looked at the boat, but, although he was a good champion and had cleverness, he did not know that he was looking at the Ocean-Sweeper, the boat that could carry any one in a moment to whatever place they wished to be; and he did not know that the old man was the Tawny Mananaun, the Son of Lear, who rules all the oceans of the world.

"Old man," said Cian, "will you row me across the waters to the land of Balor ? "

" I will row you, young champion, if you swear to give me half of what you gain there."

" I will share everything with you but the halter of Gobniu's Cow."

" I will not ask for that," said the boatman.

" Be it so," said the other. They stepped into the boat, and in a moment they touched the land of the Fomor.

" You have helped me in need, old man," said Cian. " I have a gold ring, and my cloak is rich— I pray you keep them both."

" I will change cloaks," said the old man, " but I will not take the ring." He put his hand on Cian's fingers. " I leave you a gift," he said, " whatever lock you touch will open before you. He put his cloak on Cian's shoulders. " It covers you as night covers the earth—beneath it you are safe, for no one can see you."

The cloak fell about Cian in long folds ; he knew there was magic in it and turned to look closely at the old man, but he could not see him and the boat was gone.

Cian was in a strange country, all cold, and desolate, and death-looking ; he saw fierce warriors of the Fomor, but the cloak sheltered him and he reached the court of Balor without mishap.

" What seek you of me ? " said Balor.

" I would take service with you," said Cian.

" What can you do ? "

The Cow of Plenty

"Whatever the De Danaans can do," said Cian. "I could make grass grow in this land, where grass never grew."

Balor looked pleased when he heard that, for he had the greatest desire in the world for a garth of apple trees like the apple trees Mananaun had in the Island of Avilion, that were so beautiful people made songs about them.

"Can you make apple trees grow?" said he to Cian.

"I can," said Cian.

"Well," said Balor, "make me a garth of apple trees like the garth Mananaun has; and when I see apples on the trees I will give you your own asking of reward."

"I have only one reward to ask," said Cian, "and I will ask for it at the beginning; it is the halter of Gobniu's Cow."

"I will give you that," said Balor, "without deceit."

Cian was glad when he made the bargain, and he began to work; he had his sufficiency of trouble over the grass, for every blade that grew for him in the morning was withered by Balor's breath at night. After a while he had apple trees, and as he used to be minding them he often looked at a great white dun that was near. Warriors of the Fomorians were always guarding it, and one day he asked who it was lived there.

"Ethlinn, Balor's daughter, lives there," said the man he asked. "She is the most beautiful woman in the world, but no one may see her, and she is shut in the dun lest she should marry, for it is said that a son born of her will slay Balor."

Cian kept thinking of this, and there was a wish on him to see the beautiful woman. He put the magic cloak on him and went to the dun. When he laid his hand on the door it opened, because of the enchantment on his fingers. He went in and found Balor's daughter. She was sitting at a loom, weaving a cloth that had every colour in it, and singing as she wove. Cian stood awhile looking at her till she said:

"Who is here that I cannot see?"

Then he dropped the cloak. Balor's daughter loved him when she saw him, and chose him for her man. He came to her many times after that, and they took oaths of faithfulness to one another. There was a child born to them, and he was so beautiful that whatever place he was in seemed to be full of sunshine. Ethlinn, his mother, called him Lugh, which means Light, but Cian, his father, used to call him the Sun-God; and both names stuck to him, but Lugh was the name he was best known by.

Now Balor was watching the apple trees, and when he saw apples on them he brought the halter of Gobniu's Cow to his daughter, and said:

"Hide this, and when I am asked for it, it will be gone from me."

Balor's daughter took the halter, and a little afterwards Cian came to her with a branch of apples.

"The first apples for you!" he said.

The Cow of Plenty

She gave him the halter.

" Take it--and the child, and go away to the land you came from."

" That is a hard saying ! " said Cian.

" There is nothing else to do," said she.

Cian took the child and the halter, and wrapped his cloak about him. He said farewell to Balor's daughter and went till he came to the dark waters. A boat was there before him and the old man in it. Cian thought they were a short time in crossing.

" Do you remember our bargain ? " said the old man.

" I do," said Cian, " but I have nothing but the halter and this child—I will not make two halves of him."

" I had your word on it ! " said the old man.

" I will give you the child," said Cian.

" You will never be sorry for it," said the old man, " for I will foster him and bring him up like my own son."

The boat touched the land of Ireland.

" Here is your cloak," said Cian, " and take the child."

Mananaun took the little child in his arms, and Cian put the cloak about him, and when he shook it out it had every colour of the sea in it and a sound like the waves when they break on a shore with the music of bells. The old man was beautiful and wonderful to look at, and Cian cried out to him:

" I know you now, Mananaun Mac Lear, and it was in a lucky hour I gave my son to you, for he will be brought up in Tir-nan-Oge, and will never know sorrow or defeat ! "

Mananaun laughed and lifted the little Sun-God high up in his two hands.

"When you see him again, Cian, son of Dian-Cecht, he will be riding on my own white horse and no one will bar his way on land or sea. Now, take farewell of him, and may gladness and victory be with you!"

Mananaun stepped into the boat; it was shining with every colour of the rainbow as clear as crystal, and it went without oars or sails with the water curling round the sides of it and the little fishes of the sea swimming before and behind it.

Cian set his face towards the house of Gobniu, the Smith. He came to it, and he had the halter in his hand, and when he came the Cow was there before him and Gobniu came out to meet him.

"A welcome before you, young champion, and may everything you undertake have a happy ending!"

"The same wish to yourself!" said Cian, and gave him the halter. The Smith gave Cian the sword then, and there was gladness and friendship between them ever after.

THE COMING OF LUGH

ANANAUN MAC LIR who rules the ocean took the little Sun-God, Lugh, in his arms and held him up so that he could see the whole of Ireland with the waves whispering about it everywhere.

"Say farewell to the mountains and rivers, and the big trees and the flowers in the grass, O Lugh, for you are coming away with me."

The child stretched out his hands and cried:

"Good-bye, mountains and flowers and rivers: some day I will come back to you."

Then Mananaun wrapped Lugh in his cloak and stepped into his boat, the Ocean-Sweeper, and without oar or sail they journeyed over the sea till they crossed the waters at the edge of the world and came to the country of Mananaun—a beautiful country shining with the colours of the dawn.

Lugh stayed in that country with Mananaun. He raced the waves along the strand; he gathered apples sweeter than honey from trees with crimson blossoms : and wonderful birds came to play with him. Mananaun's daughter, Niav, took him through woods where there were milk-white deer with horns of gold, and black-maned lions and spotted panthers, and unicorns that shone like silver, and strange beasts that no one ever heard of ; and all the animals were glad to see him, and he played with them and called them by their names. Every day he grew taller and stronger and more beautiful, but he did not any day ask Mananaun to take him back to Ireland.

Every night when darkness had come into the sky, Mananaun wrapped himself in his mantle of power and crossed the sea and walked all round Ireland, stepping from rock to rock. No one saw him, because his mantle made him invisible, but he saw everything and knew that trouble had found the De Danaans. The ugly, mis-shapen folk of the Fomor had come into Ireland and spread themselves over the country like a pestilence. They had stolen the Cauldron of Plenty and carried it away to their own land, where Balor of the Evil Eye reigned. They had taken the Spear of Victory also, and the only one of the four great Jewels of Sovereignty remaining to the De Danaans was the Stone of Destiny. It was hidden deep in the earth of Ireland, and because of it the Fomorians could not altogether conquer the country, nor could they destroy the De Danaans, though they drove them from

The Coming of Lugh

their pleasant palaces and hunted them through the glens and valleys like outlaws.

Mananaun himself had the fourth Jewel, the Sword of Light: he kept it and waited.

When Lugh was full grown, Mananaun said to him:

"It is three times seven years, as mortals count time, since I brought you to Tir-nan-Oge, and in all that time I have never given you a gift. To-day I will give you a gift."

He brought out the Sword of Light and gave it to Lugh, and when Lugh took it in his hand he remembered how he had cried to the hills and rivers of Ireland—"Some day I will come back to you!" And he said to Mananaun:

"I want to go back to Ireland."

"You will not find joyousness there, O Lugh, or the music of harp strings, or feasting. The De Danaans are shorn of their strength. Ogma, their Champion, carries logs to warm Fomorian hearths; Angus wanders like an outcast; and Nuada, the King, has but one dun, where those who had once the lordship of the world meet in secret like hunted folk."

"I have a good sword," said Lugh. "I will go to my kinsfolk."

"O Lugh," said Mananaun, "they have never known you. Will you leave me, and Niav, and this land where sorrow has never touched you, for the sake of stranger kinsfolk?"

Lugh answered:

"I remember the hills and the woods and the

rivers of Ireland, and though all my kinsfolk were gone from it and the sea covered everything but the tops of the mountains, I would go back."

"You have the hardiness that wins victory," said Mananaun. "I will set you on my own white horse and give you companions as high-hearted as yourself. I will put my helmet on your head and my breast-plate over your heart: you shall drive the Fomorians out of Ireland as chaff is driven by the wind."

When Lugh put on the helmet of Mananaun, brightness shot into the sky as if a new sun had risen; when he put on the breast-plate, a great wave of music swelled and sounded through Tir-nan-Oge; when he mounted the white horse, a mighty wind swept past him, and lo! the companions Mananaun had promised rode beside him. Their horses were white like his, and gladness that age cannot wither shone in their faces. When they came to the sea that is about Tir-nan-Oge, the little crystal waves lifted themselves up to look at Lugh, and when he and his comrades sped over the sea as lightly as blown foam, the little waves followed them till they came to Ireland, and the Three Great Waves of Ireland thundered a welcome—the Wave of Thoth; the Wave of Rury; and the long, slow, white, foaming Wave of Cleena.

No one saw the Faery Host coming into Ireland. At the place where their horses leaped from sea to land there was a great wood of pine trees.

"Let us go into the wood," said Lugh, and

The Coming of Lugh

they rode between the tall straight tree-trunks into the silent heart of the wood.

"Rest here," said Lugh, "till morning. I will go to the dun of Nuada and get news of my kinsfolk."

He put his shining armour from him and wrapped himself in a dark cloak and went on foot to the dun of Nuada. He struck the brazen door, and the Guardian of the Door spoke to him from within.

"What do you seek?"

"My way into the dun."

"No one enters here who has not his craft. What can you do?"

"I have the craft of a Carpenter."

"We have a carpenter within; he is Luchtae, son of Luchaid."

"I have the craft of a Smith."

"We have a smith within, Colum of the three new ways of working."

"I have the craft of a Champion."

"We have a champion within; he is Ogma himself."

"I have the craft of a Harper."

"We have a harper within, even Abhcan, son of Bicelmos; the Men of the Three Gods chose him in the faery hills."

"I have the craft of a Poet and Historian."

"We have a poet and historian within, even En, son of Ethaman."

"I have the craft of a Wizard."

"We have many wizards and magicians within."

"I have the craft of a Physician."

69

"We have a physician within, even Dian Cecht."

"I have the craft of a Cupbearer."

"We have nine cupbearers within."

"I have the craft of a Brazier."

"We have a brazier within, even Credne Cerd."

"Go hence and ask your king if he has within any one man who can do all these things. If he has, I will not seek to enter."

The Guardian of the Door hurried in to Nuada.

"O King," he said, "the most wonderful youth in the world is waiting outside your door to-night! He seeks admittance as the Ildana, the Master of Every Craft."

"Let him come in," said King Nuada.

Lugh came into the dun. Ogma, the Champion, took a good look at him. He thought him young and slender, and was minded to test him. He stooped and lifted the Great Stone that was before the seat of the King. It was flat and round, and four score yoke of oxen could not move it. Ogma cast it through the open door so that it crossed the fosse which was round the dun. That was his challenge to the Ildana.

"It is a good champion-cast," said Lugh. "I will better it."

He went outside. He lifted the Stone and cast it back—not through the door, but through the strong wall of the dun—so that it fell in the place where it had lain before Ogma lifted it.

70

The Coming of Lugh

" Your cast is better than mine ! " said Ogma.
" Sit in the seat of the champion with your face
to the King."

Lugh drew his hand over the wall; it became
whole as before.   He sat in the champion-seat.

" Let chess be brought," said the King.

They played, and Lugh won all the games,
so that thereafter it passed into a proverb " to
make the Cro of Lugh."

" Truly you are the Ildana," said Nuada.
" I would fain hear music of your making, but
I have no harp to offer you."

" I see a kingly harp within reach of your hand,"
said Lugh.

" That is the harp of the Dagda.   No one
can bring music from that harp but himself.
When he plays on it, the four Seasons—Spring,
Summer, Autumn, and Winter—pass over the
earth."

" I will play on it," said Lugh.

The harp was given to him.

Lugh played the music of joy, and outside
the dun the birds began to sing as though it
were morning and wonderful crimson flowers
sprang through the grass—flowers that trembled
with delight and swayed and touched each other
with a delicate faery ringing as of silver bells.
Inside the dun a subtle sweetness of laughter
filled the hearts of every one : it seemed to them
that they had never known gladness till that
night.

Lugh played the music of sorrow.   The wind

Celtic Wonder-Tales

moaned outside, and where the grass and flowers had been there was a dark sea of moving waters. The De Danaans within the dun bowed their heads on their hands and wept, and they had never wept for any grief.

Lugh played the music of peace, and outside there fell silently a strange snow. Flake by flake it settled on the earth and changed to starry dew. Flake by flake the quiet of the Land of the Silver Fleece settled in the hearts and minds of Nuada and his people: they closed their eyes and slept, each in his seat.

Lugh put the harp from him and stole out of the dun. The snow was still falling outside. It settled on his dark cloak and shone like silver scales; it settled on the thick curls of his hair and shone like jewelled fire; it filled the night about him with white radiance. He went back to his companions.

The sun had risen in the sky when the De Danaans awoke in Nuada's dun. They were light-hearted and joyous and it seemed to them that they had dreamed overnight a strange, beautiful dream.

"The Fomorians have not taken the sun out of the sky," said Nuada. "Let us go to the Hill of Usna and send to our scattered comrades that we may make a stand against our enemies."

They took their weapons and went to the Hill of Usna, and they were not long on it when a band of Fomorian devastators came upon them. The Fomorians scoffed among themselves when

72

The Coming of Lugh

they saw how few the De Danaans were, and how ill-prepared for fighting.

"Behold," they cried, "what mighty kings are to-day upon Usna, the Hill of Sovereignty! Come down, O Kings, and bow yourselves before your masters!"

"We will not bow ourselves before you," said Nuada, "for ye are ugly and vile : and lords neither of us nor of Ireland."

With hoarse cries the Fomorians fell on the De Danaans, but Nuada and his folk held together and withstood them as well as they were able. Scarcely had the weapons clashed when a light appeared in the horizon and a sound of mighty battle trumpets shook the air. The light was so white that no one could look at it, and great rose-red streamers shot from it into the sky.

"It is a second sunrise!" said the Fomorians.

"It is The Deliverer!" said the De Danaans.

Out of the light came the glorious company of warriors from Tir-nan-Oge. Lugh was leading them. He had the helmet of Mananaun on his head, the breast-plate of Mananaun over his heart, and the great white horse of Mananaun beneath him.

The Sword of Light was bare in his hand. He fell on the Fomorians as a sea-eagle falls on her prey, as lightning flashes out of a clear sky. Before him and his companions they were destroyed as stubble is destroyed by fire. He held his hand when only nine of them remained alive.

"Bow yourselves," he said, "before King Nuada, and before the De Danaans, for they are your Lords and the Lords of Ireland, and go hence to Balor of the Evil Eye and tell him and his mis-shapen brood that the De Danaans have taken their own again and they will wage war against the Fomorians till there is not one left to darken the earth with his shadow."

The nine Fomorians bowed themselves before King Nuada, and before the De Danaans; and before Lugh Lauve Fauda, the Ildana; and they arose and carried his message to Balor of the Evil Eye, King of the Fomorians.

THE ERIC-FINE OF LUGH

 HE chiefs of the Tuatha De Danaan thronged round Lugh on the Hill of Usna. Lugh stood on the summit, and the Sword of Light was bare in his hand: all the hill below him shone with a radiance like white silver.

"Chiefs," cried Lugh, "behold the Sword! Ye should have three great jewels to match it. Where are the Spear of Victory, the Cauldron of Plenty, and the Stone of Destiny?"

The Tuatha De Danaan bowed their heads and veiled their faces before Lugh, and answered:

"The Fomor have taken the Cauldron of Plenty and the Spear of Victory from us. Ask the Earth of Ireland for the Stone."

Lugh whirled the Sword till it became a glancing wheel of light, and cried:

"O Earth of Ireland, sacred and beloved, have you the Lia Fail, the Stone of Destiny?"

A strong sweet music welled up from the earth, and every stone and every leaf and every drop of

77

water shone with light till all Ireland seemed one vast crystal, white and shining. The white light changed to rose, as it had been a ruby ; and the ruby to sapphire ; and the sapphire to emerald ; the emerald to opal ; the opal to amethyst ; and the amethyst to diamond, white and radiant with every colour.

" It is enough ! " cried Lugh. " I am well answered : the earth of Ireland has kept the Stone."

" O Chiefs," he said, " raise up your foreheads. Though ye have not the jewels ye have the scars of battle-combat, and ye have endured sorrow and hardship for ye have known what it is to be exiles in your own land. Let us swear brotherhood now by the Sword and the Stone that we may utterly destroy the Fomor and cleanse the world. Hold up your hands and swear, as I and those who came with me from Tir-nan-Oge will swear, and as the Sacred Land will swear, that we may have one mind and one heart and one desire amongst us all."

Then the De Danaans lifted up their hands and swore a great oath of brotherhood with the Earth and with the hosts of the Shining Ones from Tir-nan-Oge. They swore by the Sword of Light and the Stone of Destiny ; by the Fire that is over the earth ; and the Fire that is under the earth ; and the Fire in the heart of heroes. They swore to have one mind, one heart, and one desire, until the Fomor should be destroyed. Lugh swore the same oath, and all his shining

The Eric-Fine of Lugh

comrades from Tir-nan-Oge swore it. The hills and valleys and plains and rivers and lakes and forests of Ireland swore it—they all fastened the bond of brotherhood on themselves.

" Let us go hence," said Lugh, when the oath was ended, " and make ready for the great battle."

At his word all the chiefs departed, each going his own road.

IAN, the father of Lugh, was crossing the plain of Louth that is called Moy Myeerhevna : he lifted up his eyes and saw the three sons of Turann coming towards him. There was black hatred between himself and the sons of Turann, and he was minded not to meet them. He took the form of a wild boar and hid himself with a herd of swine. Brian, Ur, and Urcar, the sons of Turann, saw him do it, and anger leaped in them.

" Come forth ! " they cried. " Show your face to us."

Cian did not come forth.

Ur and Urcar changed themselves into hounds and hunted the strange boar from the herd.

Brian made a cast of his spear at it, and when Cian felt the wound, he cried out:

"Hold! Brian, son of Turann: do not slay me in the form of a pig!"

"Take your own form."

Cian took his own form, and said:

"Ye see my face now, Sons of Turann, with blood on it. Well ye knew me from the first, and well I knew you—Oath-Breakers!"

"The bands of death on your poisonous tongue!" said Urcar. "Take back your word!"

"I will not take it back, Sons of the Adder. Slay me! and every drop of blood will cry out on you—your very weapons will cry out on you in the Place of Assembly."

"We will slay you with weapons that cannot cry out," said the Sons of Turann, and they lifted great stones and rocks from the earth and stoned Cian till he was dead.

The Sons of Turann buried the body of Cian the depth of a man's height in the ground, but the earth refused to hide the body and cast it up again before them. They buried it a second time, and a second time the earth refused to hide the body and cast it up before them. Six times they buried it, and six times the earth cast it up. They buried it the seventh time, and that time the earth made no sign. The body of Cian was hidden. The Sons of Turann hastened away from the place and went to the court of King Nuada to show themselves with the other warriors.

The Eric-Fine of Lugh

The earth sent a little wind to Lugh Lauve Fauda. It touched his face and eyelids; it lifted the thick curls of his hair; it touched his hand as a hound touches the hand of a beloved master, and Lugh knew the wind had come for him. He followed it till he reached the place where Cian had been slain.

"O Lugh," said the earth, "the bond of brotherhood is broken. The Sons of Turann have slain your father. Look what a poor torn thing I cover!"

The Earth laid bare the body of Cian. Lugh looked at the mangled blood-stained body, and at the trampled dishonoured earth, and in his eyes two tears slowly gathered. He shook them away, and then he saw that the earth had sent up a little well of pure water close to him. He bent over it.

"O Earth," he said, "forgive the broken bond!"

The little spring in the heart of the well leaped in answer, and nine crystal bubbles rose through the water. Lugh made a cup of his two hands and lifted water from the well. He sprinkled it on the torn earth, and greenness came again to the trampled grass. He sprinkled it on the bruised body of his father, and it became whole and white again.

"O Earth," he said, "most noble and beloved, I will avenge your wrong."

"O Father," he said, "you shall yet send help for the battle, and the hands of your slayers shall bring it. 'Tis not wearisome to wait for news of victory in Moy Mell, for all the winds that blow there are winds of beauty, and now you have the crimson flowers beneath your feet and the radiance of the Silver Fleece about you."

He laid the body of Cian tenderly in the earth and went to seek the slayers at the court of King Nuada.

UADA sat in his royal seat. There was a white light about him as it had been a fleece of silver, and round his head a wheel of light pulsed and beat with changing colours. His face was joyous and the faces of the Tuatha De Danaan were joyous. The great door of the dun was open and De Danaan chiefs came and went through it.

Lugh came into the dun and with him came such heaviness of heart that joy was shaken from the assembly.

"Why is the hero-light gone from your forehead, O Lugh, Ildana?" said Nuada.

"It is because I have seen the dead body of my father—and the earth trampled into mire and blood."

The Eric-Fine of Lugh

The light went from the head of Nuada and he veiled his face. All the chiefs bowed their heads and raised the three sorrowful cries of the keene. Only the three sons of Turann remained with haughty eyes and unbowed heads.

" O Wind of Misfortune," cried the chiefs, " that brought the Fomor at the first to us ! "

" It was not from the Fomor, O Chiefs, that Cian, Son of Dian-Cecht, got death—the hands that slew him have sworn the oath of brotherhood."

" Name his slayers ! " cried Nuada ; " and though they be our noblest and most loved— though they be even the Sons of Turann—they shall perish utterly ! "

" The slayers are the three sons of Turann ! "

Nuada looked on the three Sons of Turann, and when he saw they had no words to answer Lugh his heart failed him, for the three were the mightiest and most beautiful of his warriors and there was no one with more hero-gifts than Brian unless it were the Ildana himself.

" Let them perish ! " said Nuada.

" Nay, King of the Tuatha De Danaan," said Lugh, " let them make good the battle-loss ! Let them pay eric for the warrior they have slain ! "

" You are well named the Ildana," said the King, " for truly wisdom is with you ! " and then he said to the Sons of Turann. " Will ye make good the battle-loss ? Will ye pay eric for Cian, son of Dian-Cecht ? "

They answered : " We will pay eric : let Lugh Lauve Fauda ask it of us."

"I ask three apples, a pig-skin, a spear, a chariot with two horses, seven swine, a hound, a cooking-spit, and three shouts on a hill."

"You have stretched out your hand for a small eric-fine, Lugh the Long-Handed."

"I have not stretched out my hand for a small fine, Brian, son of Turann. The apples I ask are three golden apples from the tree that is watched by sleepless dragons in the Eastern half of the world. The skin I ask is the skin of that pig before whom rivers of water turned into rivers of wine. The skin has power to turn whatever water it touches into wine, and if it be wrapped about a man wounded to death it will give him back his life and make his body clean and whole again. It is the jewel in a great king's treasure-house, and ye will not find it easy to get. The spear I ask is the fiery victory-giver that is kept in times of peace with its head sunk in a cauldron of magic water lest it should destroy the world. The chariot I ask is the chariot of Dobar: it outshines all chariots that have been made or shall be made. The horses yoked to it do not draw back their feet from the sea-waves: their going is as lordly on the wide plain of the sea as it is on the land. The seven pigs I ask are the pigs of Asal, the King of the Golden Pillars—though they be killed and eaten to-day, they will be alive and well to-morrow, and whoso eats of them shall never know what it is to lack strength. The hound is the hound Failinis. He is brighter than the sun at mid-summer. The beasts of the forest are

The Eric-Fine of Lugh

astonished at the sight of him: they have no strength to contend against him. The cooking-spit is a guarded flame. Fifty-three women keep it in the island of Caer, in the green stillness that is under the sea-waves. The three shouts must be given on the hill that is guarded by Midkena and his sons—no champion since the beginning of time has raised a victory-shout on that hill. I have named my eric, sons of Turann. Do ye choose to pay it, or will ye humble yourselves and ask grace?"

"We will pay the eric," said the sons of Turann, and they went forth from the Court of King Nuada.

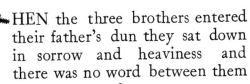 HEN the three brothers entered their father's dun they sat down in sorrow and heaviness and there was no word between them till their sister Enya came to them.

"Why does sorrow darken your faces and the faces of the household?" she asked. "What grief has come upon you?"

"We have slain Cian, son of Dian-Cecht, the father of Lugh Lauve Fauda!"

"Alas!" cried Enya, and she beat her hands

together. "Alas! ye have broken Lugh's protection out of Ireland: he will not fight in the Great Battle now!"

"Lugh will fight in the Great Battle, but he has laid on us an eric that bows us to the grave-mould."

"What eric?"

"He asks the Hound Failinis; and the Spear of Victory—he asks the Seven Treasures of the World!"

"We are undone!" said Enya. "Destruction has come upon us!"

While she spoke they heard the approaching footsteps of those who attended Turann.

"Let us go," said Urcar, "before our father sees that good days are gone from us."

"Sorrow cannot be hidden," said Enya.

Turann came into the room. He was old and his strength was withered. His sons led him to the high-seat, and when he looked on them he knew an evil thing had befallen.

"Tell me," he said, "what misfortune has come to us."

Then Brian told the story of Cian's death and what eric Lugh had bound on them. When he made an end of telling it, Turann said:

"Bitter indeed to me is the coming of the Deliverer, for he has taken from me my three sons—my Three Eagles that never failed to carry off a prey, my Three Salmon of Knowledge that could make paths for themselves in all the rivers of the world, my Three Strong Bulls that stamped on the necks of kings. It is a bitter thing to be old without my sons."

" O my Father," said Brian, " if you have bred strong sons they will set forth strongly, and it may be they will bring back the eric-spoil. Do not make a lamentation for us till we are dead ! "

" Nay," said Turann, " ye are setting forth on an adventure that knows no ending, for the treasures that ye seek are hidden in the caves of dragons and under the sea-waves. Strange kings will make a mock of you leaning over battlements of adamant and strange monsters will crush your bones. Ye will not come back to me, living or dead. No one will heap the grave-mound over your bodies ! "

" O my Father," said Enya, " the heart of Lugh is set on the eric-fine. His hands are fain to grasp the fiery spear and he would see the spoils of the world brought into Ireland. Let us ask him for help. If he will give Mananaun's boat, the Ocean-Sweeper, it will not be hard for good warriors to come by the treasures—since, at a word, the Ocean-Sweeper will bear those who sit in it to whatsoever place they desire to be."

" We will ask nothing from Lugh Lauve Fauda ! " said Turann's sons.

" But I will ask ! " said Turann, and he cried aloud :

" Let my horses be yoked and my chariot made ready ! I will not sleep till I have spoken with Lugh Lauve Fauda."

Celtic Wonder-Tales

HEN Turann came to Lugh and asked for the boat, Lugh said: " Bid your sons to make ready and set forth. When they come to the edge of the sea and their feet touch the sea-foam, Mananaun's boat will be there waiting for them."

Turann hurried home with the good answer, and his sons made ready to set forth. Their kinsfolk and the swordsmen of their father's clan went with them to the edge of the sea and when their feet touched the sea-foam they saw a little boat, such as might fit one person, waiting for them.

" Lugh has deceived us ! " cried Brian. " This is not Mananaun's boat ! "

" O Brother," said Enya, " the Ocean Sweeper has as many shapes as the cloak of Mananaun has colours. Step into the boat."

When Brian had taken his place in the boat there was plenty of room, and when all the three were seated there was plenty of room, and the boat began to shine like a white crystal and the waves made a song of greeting as they lapped about the prow."

" Farewell ! " said the sons of Turann ; " keep gladness in your hearts till we come back."

The Ocean-Sweeper sprang from the shore like a sea-bird and wheeled and circled in the foam, waiting the word of command.

" Go to the Garden of the Golden Apple Tree

The Eric-Fine of Lugh

that is guarded by dragons in the Eastern Half of the World," said Brian, and the Ocean-Sweeper sped swiftly forth.

The Garden of the Golden Apple Trees was very far off, and as they went to it the sons of Turann took counsel as to how they should get the apples.

"Let two of us," said Urcar, "make good sword's play on the dragons whilst the third gathers the apples."

"Yes," said Ur, "and when the apples are got, we three will slay the dragons and fight our way out of the garden."

"Wisdom is not in your words," said Brian, "we three would leave our bones among the dragons. Let us change ourselves into hawks and swoop on the apples from above."

"That is good," said the others. And when they were come to the garden they rose in the air, three golden hawks, and swooping on the tree took each an apple. The dragons were powerless to hinder them, but three of the maidens that walked in the garden—and each one was a king's daughter—changed themselves into fierce sharp-clawed griffins and followed the hawks. They could not overtake the hawks : and when they saw that, they held themselves motionless in the air and great flashes of light came from their angry eyes. They blew out three streams of fire after the hawks. The hawks plunged into the water and became three salmon, and when they reached the Ocean-Sweeper they leaped into it and took their own shapes.

"It is well we have the Apples of Healing," said Ur, " the witchfire has burnt us to the bone ! "

They healed themselves with the apples and set out to seek the other treasures. It is long and long they were seeking them. They had foam of the Eastern World and foam of the Western World under their prow. They saw the Stars of the North and the Stars of the South and the Stars that are under the Sea. They were searching through the blackness of night and the redness of dawn and all the colours of the day. They knew the singing wave that lifts adventurers to the heights of the world and the silent wave that casts them down to the hollows. It is long they were seeking the treasures.

They got the Spear of Victory. They got the Magic Skin. They got the Hound. They got the Seven Swine. They got the Chariot. Their hearts were filled with pride and stubbornness.

Lugh, walking in Ireland by the sea, knew that the sons of Turann had the treasures, and he thought that they could too easily give the shouts on Midkena's hill and be free of the eric-fine. He made a spell of forgetfulness to bring them back and take from their minds the memory of Midkena's hill.

He stooped to lay the spell on the sea, and as he stooped a wave broke over his hands and a broken water-reed tangled itself in his fingers. He lifted up the reed and straightened it. He remembered the little well with the nine crystal bubbles, and the tenderness of the earth came into his heart.

The Eric-Fine of Lugh

"O little reed," he said, "I will give the sons of Turann a chance. I will make another spel : and if, when it reaches them, they remember the wrong they did the Earth, they will remember also the shouts on Midkena's hill."

He made a spell that had memory and forgetfulness in it and laid it on the sea, and it became a wave and travelled unbroken till it reached the boat of Mananaun. It rocked the boat softly, and the three sons of Turann remembered their father s house, but they had no sorrow for the wrong done to the earth, and forgetfulness of Midkena's hill came upon them.

"A good welcome would we have now if we were in our father's house," said Brian, "and good would it be in the morning to slip our hounds for the chase."

"And good would it be in the evening," said Urcar, " to hear the sound of harps in our father's house. Let us go back to Ireland."

"Go back to Ireland," said Brian to the Ocean-Sweeper, and it leaped through the sea-foam towards the Sacred Land.

N a height that looked far over the sea stood Turann's watcher, his eyes on the horizon. Day and night, since the setting forth of Turann's sons, a watcher had stood there, looking seaward. Swift runners waited for his joy-shout, and beacon-fires stood ready for the flame. It was early morning, and the watcher saw the pale mists whiten and the sea stir itself and wrinkle. Suddenly a great star rose in the horizon—it flashed; and grew; and neared. The watcher knew the Ocean-Sweeper. He leaped high for gladness of heart, and shouted:

"They come! They come! Turann's sons are returning!"

The cry was caught by the runners. They leaped and ran, and the joy-fires leaped and sparkled, blood-red in the paleness of morning. The joy-shout spread from mouth to mouth, and all that country rejoiced at the home-coming.

Turann went down to the edge of the sea to greet his sons, and Enya went with him and all the folk of the clan. Right glad were the three brothers to set their feet on Irish land. They showed the strange spoils, the marvellous eric-fine they had brought for Lugh, and all that saw them wondered.

News of the home-coming was sent to Lugh by swift messengers, and he said:

The Eric-Fine of Lugh

" Let the sons of Turann come and count the eric-fine before me."

The sons of Turann came before him, and with them came singing men and singing women and swordsmen and chariots and horsemen.

Brian counted out the eric-fine before Lugh.

Then Lugh said: " Good are the things ye have brought, but ye have not brought the full eric. Where is the cooking-spit that is a flame under the sea-wave ? "

Then recollection came upon the sons of Turann, and they cried out:

" We are undone ! We have not given the Shouts on Midkena's hill—we have not the Flame that is under the sea-wave ! "

Shame burnt in the faces of all their kinsfolk because the sons of Turann had not the full eric, and they said :

" Give the Ocean-Sweeper again, O Lugh, and the sons of Turann will pay the eric in full."

" Nay," said Lugh, " I lent the boat at first that the battle-loss of Cian might be made good in the great fight. The loss is made good." He bent his eyes on the sons of Turann, and said : " Ye are here now because my spell has brought you. I laid a spell of forgetfulness upon the sea, but the earth put with it a spell of remembrance, and if ye had remembered the wrong ye did the Earth, ye would have remembered the shouts on Midkena's hill, and easily would ye have given them since ye had the Spear of Victory, the Skin of Healing, and the Apples of Life. Now ye must fare forth without these treasures and without the boat of Mananaun, and whatsoever ye win ye will win solely by the strength that is in yourselves."

Then said Brian: " It is well named you are, Lugh the Long-Handed. Your vengeful fingers have reached across the sea to grasp us, and they will not loose their hold till you have dragged us under the grave-mound ! "

Turann would have spoken, but Brian said to him :

" Words are wasted, my Father; let us go."

Sorrowfully they went homeward, and their thoughts were on the pathless sea.

Turann made ready a boat for his sons; thick-planked and strong, a boat with crimson sails. He proffered them rowers and men at arms, but they refused, because they were going they knew not whither, and were under a curse.

They stepped into the boat, they spread the crimson sails, and as they slid away from the land, all their people made lamentation for them.

" The Eagles are going ! " they wailed. " The High Noble-hearted Ones, the Three Flames on the hearth of Turann. The lights are quenched to-night in the chieftain's house ! "

The Eric-Fine of Lugh

HE sons of Turann went searching for the Island of Caer, the Land that is under the Sea-Wave. They heard tidings of it in many places, but no one knew where it could be found. Wise Druids told them that the Island was protected by the magic of Fand, the Sea-Queen, the daughter of Flidias, and no one who went there ever returned.

The sun had risen and set many times on the search. Brian, Urcar and Ur were weary; the wind had failed them, and they were labouring at the oars: it seemed to them that they would never find the Island of Caer.

"Let us rest a little," said Urcar, "for my strength is spent."

They rested from the oars, and Brian cast a line over the side of the boat. He drew up a fish, white as silver and covered with crimson spots.

"Brother," said Ur, "your fish is purple-spotted like the Salmon that swims in Connla's Well and eats the crimson nuts of the Hazel of Knowledge: let him go free for sake of his beauty."

Brian threw the fish back to the water, and suddenly knowledge came to him, and he cried: "I know that the Island of Caer is beneath us!"

He jumped into the water and became a white stone, falling, falling, till he reached the Land that is Under the Sea. It was a goodly land and Brian took his own shape and walked through its starry meadows till he came to the Palace of the Guarded Flame. He entered it and found many beautiful maidens singing and broidering golden flowers on mantles for the daughter of Flidias. In the midst of them leaped and shone the Guarded Flame. Brian spoke no word when he entered and the maidens did not lift their eyes to look at him. He took the flame in his two hands and turned to leave the palace. The maidens burst out laughing.

" You are a brave man," they said, " and since the flame does not burn you, keep it. We have a flame for every day in the year, and you are the bravest champion and the handsomest that ever came to look at us broidering cloaks for the sea-queen."

" O Maidens," said Brian, " may every day in the year bring you fresh laughter and delight, and if good wishes can reach you from the country above the sea-floor ye will have mine every day I live, and farewell now, and my thousand blessings with you !"

He rose through the water till he came to where his brothers were and climbed into the boat. When the Flame came above the water it changed into a cooking-spit, and Brian laid it carefully in the boat.

" Our luck," he said, " is like sunshine in mid-winter, soon come, soon gone. Let us hasten to Midkena's Hill."

The Eric-Fine of Lugh

IDKENA'S HILL was very high and green. It rose almost straight out of the sea. Only on one side could it be climbed. On that side Midkena and his three sons were.

It was a great fight that the sons of Turann made with the Champions of the Hill. They were like fierce eagles contending together, and like bulls whose tramplings shake the earth. The demons of the air and the fierce creatures that live under the earth gathered to watch them fighting—and no one ever travelled over the nine ridges of the world to look at a fight that was better than that fight. Brian and his brothers got the victory over Midkena and his sons. They left them dead on the hill, but they themselves had barely strength to give the three shouts. When they had given the shouts weakness came on them, and they fell down and could not rise. Then Ur saw the demons of the air that have no pity and the fierce ones from under the earth watching him, and he said:

"O my brothers, I would we were in our own country, lying on a hill-side there, for the Irish hills are gentle, and every wind that blows on them is full of peace."

"We have no part in Ireland," said Brian, "for we have broken the Great Oath."

97

"My grief!" said Urcar. "My bitter sorrow that we shall never see the Sacred Land again!"

While he spoke, a little wind came out of Ireland. It was very soft and gentle. It touched the sons of Turann, and there was so much healing in its touch that they rose up and stood on their feet.

"It is a wind surely from Ireland that has come to us," said Urcar, "let us make haste while we have strength and get to the boat."

They got down to the boat. They took the fastenings from it. They hoisted slowly the crimson sails, and the little wind strengthened itself and filled the sails and kept the boat before it till the hills of Ireland showed themselves like pale clouds.

"My blessing on the hills!" said Brian, and because he had the most strength he lifted up his brothers to get sight of the Irish land.

"It is good," they said, "to see Ben Edair: our eyes were never more glad of it, and let us steer now to the haven where our father's house is."

Turann's watcher saw them afar off and raised the shout for them, and their kinsfolk and comrades waded into the sea and drew the boat to land. They lifted up the sons of Turann and would have carried them into their father's dun, but Brian said to them:

"Lay us all three on the green grass, for we are hurt past any hope of healing, and send swift runners for Lugh that we may say to him before we die: 'The sons of Turann have paid you the full eric.'"

The three were laid on the green grass, and

The Eric-Fine of Lugh

Enya, their sister, tended them, and the leeches and healers of their clan ministered unto them. Turann, their father, sat on the earth beside them : he was putting together, in his mind, words to say to Lugh.

When Lugh came, he was so fair and had such radiance about him that it seemed to every one he must have come newly out of Tir-nan-Oge.

Turann bowed himself before Lugh, and said :

" O Mighty One, my sons have paid your eric in full, and never since the mountains lifted their heads above the waters has such an eric been asked for or paid. Grant now the Skin of Healing, that my sons may live."

Lugh came to where the sons of Turann were lying. He looked at them. There was neither pity nor anger in his face.

" My brothers," he said, " life is either a king's robe or a beggar's cloak. Do ye desire to live ? "

The sons of Turann raised themselves and their hero-souls came back to them, so that they stood on their feet and cared not for their wounds.

" Ildana," they said, " we salute you ! Win victory for us in the Great Battle even as you will win it for Cian. We do not covet the beggar's robe."

They turned and took farewell of their father, and their sister, and their kinsfolk. And they knelt and kissed the sacred earth, and said :

" O Father, and O kinsfolk, entreat forgiveness for us from the earth, and friendly burial—even as we now entreat it for ourselves. Farewell. Make no lamentation for us."

But Turann and all his folk made a great lamentation.

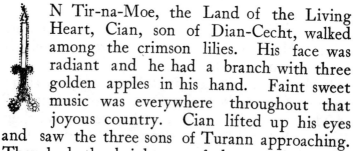

N Tir-na-Moe, the Land of the Living Heart, Cian, son of Dian-Cecht, walked among the crimson lilies. His face was radiant and he had a branch with three golden apples in his hand. Faint sweet music was everywhere throughout that joyous country. Cian lifted up his eyes and saw the three sons of Turann approaching. They had the brightness of the morning about them and there was no wound on them. Cian went to meet them.

"Greeting," he said "and welcome to Moy Mell."

He gave to each of them a golden apple. And when Brian, Ur, and Urcar had tasted of those apples they knew everything that had ever happened in the world and everything that would happen. They knew that the Fomor would be

The Eric-Fine of Lugh

defeated in the Great Battle : they knew the
words of the Peace-Chant that Brigit would sing :

> *" Peace up to Heaven,*
> *Heaven down to earth.*
> *The earth under Heaven.*
> *Strength to every one."*

" O Cian, dear Comrade," said the sons of
Turann, " it is not hard to wait for news of
victory in Moy Mell."

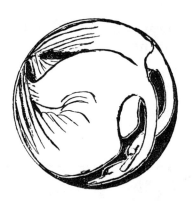

THE GREAT BATTLE

T Samhain-time, the Dagda, Ogma, and
Nuada sat together in the place that
is called the Plain of Assembly. It
was early in the day and the dew
was still on the grass. They saw
Angus coming towards them. His hair was
wound about two discs of shining gold, and
he had on a cloak the colour of an amethyst:
as he walked he brushed the dew in little pearls
from the grass. The Pooka trotted beside him
in the shape of a spotted fawn. Angus was
singing :—

> " *Ships are sailing*
> *O'er height and hollow ;*
> *Sea-hounds, sea-hounds,*
> *Lift your heads and follow.*"

" Why are you so merry ? " asked the Dagda.
" Because I have good news ! " said Angus.
" The People of the Fomor are coming in black-

hulled ships. Balor has sworn to tow the Sacred
Land behind him and drop it into the blackness
of the sea !"

> "*I had a thousand ships and ten*
> *The sea-waves kissed my feet.*"

"Angus !" said the Dagda, "I think your
mirth unseemly."

"Lugh didn't—he only laughed."

"Where did you see Lugh ?" asked Ogma.

"I saw him near the Wood of Femen. He
had a great white hound straining in a leash—
a war-dog. There will be good hunting when
the Fomor show themselves. Come, Pooka !"

The Pooka skipped up to him, and Angus went
away singing :—

> "*I had a white hound crowned with gold,*
> *Three Champions sought him over sea ;*
> *O, he'll be young when the world is old,*
> *Following, following me.*"

"Sound the great War-Horn !" said Nuada,
" so that all may know to prepare for the battle."

Ogma put the mighty trumpet to his lips and
blew a champion-blast. When the echoes of it
died away, the Three Waves thundered round
Ireland.

"Look at the hills !" said the Dagda.

A glancing flame shone like a jewel on the forehead of every hill in Ireland.

"The earth remembers the Oath," said Ogma.

The Great Battle

At the sound of the mighty trumpet, the Tuatha De Danaan hurried to the Plain of Assembly. Gobniu the Smith came, and Diancecht the Great Healer, and Airmid the druidess, and Miach, who had the secret of life. Lugh came, with the shining host from Tir-nan-Oge : they made a radiance in the assembly. Bove Darrig came, and Midyir the Haughty, and Luchtna, and Credne, and harpers came from the faery hills, and cup-bearers and magicians.

"What help will you give in the battle ? " asked Lugh, of Mathgen the Magician.

" I have power " said Mathgen, " to roll the mountains and high hills of Ireland on the Fomor. I will grind them as corn is ground between two stones. The twelve most royal mountains in Ireland will fight for you : Slieve League, Slieve Snechtai, Maccu Belgodon, Denna Ulad, Bri Ruri, Slemish, Blai Slieve, Nemthann, The Curlieu Hills, Crauchan Aigle, The Mourne Mountains, and the Mountains of Slieve Bloom."

" What help will you give ? " asked Lugh, of the Cup-Bearers.

" We will put a burning thirst on the Fomor, and the lakes and rivers of Ireland will refuse to give them water. Though they should go to Loch Luimnigh, Derg-loch, Lough Corrib, Lough Ree, Lough Mask, Strangford Lough, Lough Laeig, Lough Neagh, Lough Foyle, Lough Gara, Lough Reagh, and Murloch, the twelve most royal lakes, they would not find in any one a single drop of water to quench their thirst.

Though they should go to every river in Ireland, and supplicate the twelve that are most royal: the Bush, the Boyne, the Baa, the Nem, the Lee, the Shannon, the Moy, the Sligo, the Erne, and the Finn, they would not get from them a mouthful of water; but the Tuatha De Danaan will get water and refreshment and strength and delight from every well and lake and river in Ireland."

"What help will you give?" asked Lugh, of Figol.

"I," said Figol, the Son of Mamos, "will cause showers of druid fire to fall on the Fomor. I will wither the strength in their bodies—they shall be as green leaves shrivelled by flame. But the men of Ireland shall have the fire of youth in them—they shall be like green leaves breaking out in the Spring time."

"What help will you give?" asked Lugh, of the enchantress Dianan and the enchantress Bechulle. They said:

"We will put enchantment on withered sticks and on sods of grass and on the stones of the earth, and they will become a terror to the Fomor. They will become a multitudinous bewildering host."

"What help will you give?" asked Lugh, of Carpre the poet, son of Etain; and Carpre said:

"I will stand on the top of a mountain before sunrise. I will have in my hands a thorn of cursing and a stone of malediction. The wind will be blowing from the north and I will have my back to a thorn tree. I will make a satire on the Fomor. They will wish to hide their faces from that satire, and because of it they will have no heart to stand up against warriors."

"What help will you give ? " asked Lugh, of Gobniu.

" I will make sharp-biting swords," said Gobniu, " and spears that know the death-thrust. My weapons do not ask for themselves a second blow, a second thrust. It is more than Dolb the smith of the Fomor can say."

" And I," said Credne the brass-cerd, " I will make rivets for spears, and hilts for swords, and bosses for shields."

" And I," said Luchta, " will make spear-shafts and shield-grips."

" And I," said Diancecht, " will heal every man who has not lost the breath of life."

The Dagda had been sitting quiet all this time, lacing a thong into his brogues. He stood up now and shook out the nine folds of his cloak.

" All that each one of you has promised, loud mouthed," said the Dagda, " I will do myself, single-handed ! "

" 'Tis yourself is the Good God ! " said the others, and they let three shouts of laughter out of them.

Celtic Wonder-Tales

HE coming of the Fomor was terrible. They were multitudinous as grains of sand ; multitudinous as waves in a sea-storm. A wind of death went before them and darkness covered them. The Tuatha De Danaan drew brightness to themselves and went into the battle. Lugh did not go into the battle, because it was known that Balor would not fight till near the end.

Lugh waited for Balor. He sat on a great hill, and below him the hosts contended. He saw the spears of the Tuatha De Danaan fly like fiery rain, and those of the Fomor like hissing sleet ; and in the hissing sleet and fiery rain the demons of the air screamed and fought. At times the Fomor drove back the Tuatha De Danaan. At times the Tuatha De Danaan prevailed against the Fomor : it was so until the night came and put an end to fighting.

There was no brightness on the Tuatha De Danaan when they drew themselves out of the conflict : they were wounded and weary, and Airmid, Diancecht, and Miach, went among them with herbs of healing. It was vexation of spirit to look on the grievousness of their wounds.

Suddenly a delicate sweet music sounded in the air and the Tuatha De Danaan saw Brigit

The Great Battle

coming to them. She towered to the heavens and her mantle swept the ground like a purple mist. Her hair was plaited in nine loosened locks, and in each lock of the nine a star glittered. Wrapped in a corner of her mantle she held a crystal ball, clear as a dew-drop.

"Hail, Brigit, the Battle-Queen!" cried the warriors, but those who were wounded and nigh to death, cried:—

"Hail, Dana, the Mighty Mother!"

Brigit smiled, and a soft radiance filled the night.

"I bring you a gift," she said, and she shook the crystal drop from her mantle. When it touched the earth it became a deep clear lake.

"It is a lake from Tir-na-Moe," said Brigit, "and there is healing in it for all weariness and all battle-wounds—it will even give back life to the dead."

The Tuatha De Danaan bathed in the lake and rose out of the water joyous and radiant. At day-break they leaped to the battle, and as they went they drew down little fleecy clouds from the sky, and the clouds became shining helmets of protection to them. Terrible was the battle that day. The Fomor transformed themselves into huge serpents and scaly dragons and shapeless abominations writhing in poisonous spume. The Tuatha De Danaan drove in on them like fire that is fanned by tempest. They stabbed the twisting monstrosities as light stabs darkness— yet they could not utterly destroy them, and the battle swayed uncertain till night came.

Celtic Wonder-Tales

Through the night the Tuatha De Danaan rested and bathed in the lake from Tir-na-Moe. Strength and healing came to them. At dawn they leaped to the battle. Stupendous was the conflict. Twice the Fomor broke before the Tuatha De Danaan. Once the Tuatha De Danaan broke before the Fomor. They were like waves contending—like Fire and Water striving for mastery. Terrible was the devastation, and in the midst of it a shout went up:

" Balor ! Balor ! Balor Beimann ! Balor of the Mighty Blows ! "

Balor heaved himself against the horizon, a mighty bulk, and the Fomor gave their strength to him and their fierceness so that no power remained in them, and because of that Balor towered to the heavens and his shadow darkened half the sky.

The Tuatha De Danaan cried aloud on Lugh.

"Lugh ! Lugh ! Lugh Lauve Fauda ! Strike for us, Long-Handed son of Cian ! Strike, Ildana ! "

Lugh leaped to his feet. The Tuatha De Danaan gave him their strength and their fierceness so that he towered to the heavens, and his brightness was more terrible than the brightness of the sun at noonday.

Swift was the advance of Lugh, the Sun-Hawk. Swift was the advance of Balor, the Hooded Vulture of Night. Lugh shouted in a voice that echoed exultant to the stars. Balor shouted in a voice that shook the depths of the Abyss. Lugh gathered his strength and the strength of the

The Great Battle

Tuatha De Danaan into the Spear of Victory which he held in his hand. Balor gathered his strength and the strength of the Fomor into his mighty death-dealing Eye. He raised the baleful lid, but before the gleam that could destroy the world shot forth from it, Lugh hurled the Spear. It struck and entered the Evil Eye as fire enters a dark cavern. The strength of Lugh and all the gods of light went with it. Balor trembled; the strength that was bound up in him loosened; his huge bulk wavered and became a shadow, and the shadow melted and became a shapeless gloom.

In the shapeless gloom something glittered. It was the Sword of Tethra, the Great Sword of the Abyss. Lugh swooped upon it, and as he lifted it the Tuatha De Danaan pressed behind him and before him and about him and scattered the darkness and drew into themselves the fierceness and might of the Fomor so that they were girt with the powers of Night and Day.

The Sword of Tethra, the Great Sword of the Abyss, was given to Ogma. He drew it from its sheath. The sunshine ran along the blade like a river of light, and the spirits that live under the sliding green waves of the sea and the spirits of the storm-wind shouted for joy. Ogma held the Sword aloft, and thunderous music broke over the earth and died away among the stars. Then Brigit, the Mor Reegu, the Battle-Queen that is called Dana, cried out to the hills and lakes and rivers and woods and valleys and plains of

Celtic Wonder-Tales

Ireland the news of victory. This is the Peace-
Chant she made :--

> " *Peace up to Heaven,*
> *Heaven down to Earth ;*
> *The Earth under Heaven*
> *Strength to every one.*"

INISFAIL

IT was on the First of May that the Milesians came into Ireland. They came with their wives and their children and all their treasures. There were many of them. They came in ships, and it is said by some that they came from a land beyond the utmost blueness of the sky and that their ships left the track among the stars that can still be seen on winter nights.

When they were come to Ireland they drew up their ships. They put the fastening of a year and a day on them and set foot on the Sacred Land. Amergin was the first to set foot on the Land, and he made this rann in honour of it. He chanted the rann because he was the chief poet and druid among the Milesians.

THE RANN.

I am The Wind That Blows Over The Sea,
    Ah-ro-he !
I am The Wave Of The Sea,
    Ah-ro-he !

117

I am The Sound The Sea Makes,
Ah-ro-he !
I am The Ox Of The Seven Combats,
Ah-ro-he !
I am The Vulture Upon The Rock,
Ah-ro-he !
I am The Ray Of The Sun,
Ah-ro-he !
I am The Fairest Of Plants,
Ah-ro-he !
I am The Wild Boar,
Ah-ro-he !
I am The Salmon In The Water,
Ah-ro-he !
I am The Lake In The Plain,
Ah-ro-he !
I am The Word Of Knowledge,
Ah-ro-he !
I am The Spear-Point Of Battle,
Ah-ro-he !
I am The God Who Kindles Fire In The Head,
Ah-ro-he !
Who makes wise the company on the mountain ?
Who makes known the ages of the moon ?
Who knows the secret resting-place of the sun ?
Ah-ro-he !

The Milesians gave a victory-shout at the end of the rann, and Amergin said:

"We will go forward now, and when we reach the place where it seems good to rest we will light a fire and put Three Names of Power on the Land so that it may belong to us for ever."

Inisfail

They went forward then and they saw no one till Brigit took the shape of a woman that has known hardship, and came to try them. She wrapped herself in the cloak of Sorrow and sat by the roadside. She made a great keening.

" O woman," said Amergin, " why is there such heavy sorrow on you, and why do you make such a shrill keening ? "

" I am keening lost possessions, and lost queenship, and a name cried down the wind of change and forgotten."

" Whose name is cried down the wind ? "

" The name of Banba that was queen of this land."

" Her name shall not be whirled into forgetfulness. I will put it on this land : it shall be called Banba."

" My blessing on you, Stag with Golden Horns, and may the name-giving bring you luck ! "

So Amergin gave away the First Name.

They went on from that place, and Brigit took the shape of a fierce beautiful queen that has lost a battle, and came again to try them.

" O Queen," said Amergin, " may all the roads of the world be pleasant to you ! "

" O King," said Brigit, " all the roads of the world are hard when those who were wont to go in chariots walk barefoot on them."

" O Queen," said Amergin, " I would fain better your fortune."

" Grant me then a queen's asking."

" Name your asking."

" I am Eriu, wife of Mac Grian, Son of the Sun, and I would have my name fastened on this land for ever."

" I will put your name on this land : it shall be called Eriu."

" My blessing on you, Sun-Crested Eagle, and may the name-giving bring you luck ! "

So Amergin gave away the Second Name.

They went on from that place, and Brigit took the form of an old wrinkled crone bent double with age, and came again to try them. She was gathering sticks, and the bundle was heavy.

" O woman," said Amergin, " it is hard to see you lifting a bundle when age has bent you so low already. I would fain better your fortune."

Brigit raised herself, and said :—

" Though I am an old crone now, bent and withered, yet I was once a great queen, and I will take nothing less than a queen's asking from you."

" What is your asking ? "

" Let my name be on this land : I am Fiola."

" I will put your name on this land : it shall be called Fiola."

" My blessing on you, Silver-Spotted Salmon of Knowledge, and may the name-giving bring you luck ! "

So Amergin gave away the Third Name.

It was after that they made a fire for themselves, and when the smoke of it rose against the sky, Ogma, Nuada, and the Dagda, came to try them.

"What people are you ? " asked Nuada, " and from what country have you come ? "

"We are the sons of Milesius," they answered ; " he himself is the son of a god—even of Beltu, the Haughty Father. We are come from Moy More, the Great Plain that is beyond the horizon of the world."

"How got you knowledge of Ireland ? " asked Ogma.

"O Champion," answered Amergin, " from the centre of the Great Plain there rises a tower of crystal. Its top pierces the heavens, and from the ramparts of it the wisest one among us got sight of this land. When he saw it his heart was filled with longing, and when he told us of it our hearts too were filled with longing. Therefore we set out to seek that land, and behold we have come to it. We have come to Inisfail, the Island of Destiny."

"And ye have come to it," said the Dagda, " like thieves in the night ; without proclamation ; without weapon-challenge. Ye have lighted a fire here, as if this were a no-man's land. Judge ye if this be hero conduct."

"Your words have the bitterness of truth in them," said Amergin. " Say now what you would have us do."

"You are a druid and a leader among your people," said Nuada. " Give judgment, there-fore, between yourselves and us."

"I will give judgment," said Amergin "I judge it right that we should return to our ships and go out the distance of nine waves from the land. Use all your power against us, and we will use all our power against you. We will take the Island of Destiny by the strength of our hands, or die fighting for it!"

"It is a good judgment," said Ogma, "Get back to your ships! We will gather our battle-chiefs for the fight."

Ogma, Nuada, and the Dagda, went away then from the Milesians.

The Milesians began to put out the fire they had kindled, and as they were quenching the embers, Brigit threw her mantle of power about her and came to the Milesians in her own shape. When Amergin saw her he knew that she was the Mighty Mother, and he cried out:

"O Ashless Flame, put a blessing on us now, that our luck may not be extinguished with these embers."

"O Druid," said Brigit, "if you had wisdom you would know that before the First Fire is extinguished the name-blessing should be pronounced over it."

"O Mother of All Wisdom, I know it, but the name-blessing is gone from me. I met three queens as I came hither, and each one asked the name-gift of me. They were queens discrowned: I could not put refusal on them."

Brigit began to laugh then, and she cried:

"O Amergin, you are not counted a fool,

Inisfail

yet it seems to me that if you had much
wit you would know the eyes of Brigit under
any cloak in the world. It was I, myself, who
asked the name-gift from you three times,
and got it   Do not ask a fourth blessing from
me now, for I have blessed you three times
already."

She stooped and lifted a half-quenched ember
from the fire. She blew on it till it became a
golden flame—till it became a star. She tossed
it from one hand to the other as a child tosses a
ball. She went away laughing.

The Milesians went back to their ships. They
put the distance of nine waves between themselves and the land. The Tuatha De Danaan
loosed the Fomor on them, and a mighty tempest
broke about their ships. Great waves leaped over
them and huge abysses of water engulped them.
The utmost power of the Milesians could not
bring the ships a hair's breadth nearer to the
shore. A terrible wind beat on them. Ireland
disappeared. Then Amergin cried out:

"O Land, that has drawn us hither, help us!
Show us the noble fellowship of thy trees: we
will be comrades to them. Show us the shining
companies of thy rivers: we will put a blessing
on every fish that swims in them. Show us thy
hero-hearted mountains: we will light fires
of rejoicing for them. O Land, help us! help
us! help us!"

Ireland heard him, and sent help. The darkness cleared away and the wind was stilled.

Celtic Wonder-Tales

Then Amergin said:

"O Sea, help us! O mighty fruitful Sea! I call on every wave that ever touched the land. O Sea, help us!"

The sea heard him, and the three waves that go round Ireland—the wave of Thoth, the wave of Rury and the long slow white foaming wave of Cleena. The three waves came and lifted the ships to the shore. The Milesians landed. The Tuatha De Danaan came down to make trial of their battle-strength. Hard was the contest between them. The Milesians held their own against the gods. When they saw that the Milesians could hold their own, the Tuatha De Danaan drew themselves out of the fight. They laughed and cried to the Milesians:

"Good heroes are ye, and worthy to win the earth: we put our blessing on you."

Nuada shook the bell-branch, and the glory that the Tuatha De Danaan had in Tir-na-Moe before they ever set themselves to the shaping of the earth—that glory—came back to them. They had such splendour that the Milesians veiled their eyes before them.

"Do not veil your eyes!" said Nuada, "we will draw the Cloak of Invisibility, the Faed Feea, about us. We give you Ireland: but, since our hands have fashioned it, we will not utterly leave the country. We will be in the white mist that clings to the mountains; we will be the quiet that broods on the lakes; we will be the joy-shout of the rivers; we will be the secret wisdom of the woods. Long after your descendants have forgotten us, they will hear our music on sunny raths and see our great white horses lift their heads from the mountain-tarns and shake the night-dew from their crested manes: in the end they will know that all the beauty in the world comes back to us, and their battles are only echoes of ours. Lift up your faces, Children of Milesius, Children of Beltu the Haughty Father, and greet the land that belongs to you ! "

The Milesians lifted up their heads. No glory blinded them, for the Tuatha De Danaan had drawn the Faed Feea about themselves. They saw the sunlight on the grass like emerald fire ; they saw the blueness of the sky and the solemn darkness of the pine trees ; they heard the myriad sound of shaken branches and running water, and behind it echoed the laughter of Brigit.

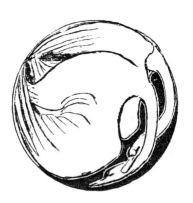

THE GOLDEN FLY

THAUN, Angus, Fuamach, and Midyir lived in the World of the Gods. Ethaun said to Angus:

" I am weary of everything that I see ; let me go into the other worlds with you."

Angus said :

" When I go into the other worlds I wander from place to place and people do not know that I am a god. In the earth they think I am a juggler or a wandering minstrel or a beggar-man. If you come with me you will seem a poor singing woman or a strolling player."

Then Ethaun said :

" I will ask Midyir to make a world for myself— all the worlds are full of weariness."

She went to find Midyir, and as she went she saw below her the World of the Bright Shadow that is called Ildathach, and the World of the Dark Shadow that is called Earth. Midyir was looking down at the Earth, and a brightness grew on it as he looked. Ethaun was angry because

Midyir cared to make a brightness on the Earth, and she turned away from him, and said:

"I wish the worlds would clash together and disappear! I am weary of everything I can see."

Then Fuamach said:

"You have the heart of a fly, that is never contented; take the body of a fly, and wander till your heart is changed and you get back your own shape again."

Ethaun became a little golden fly, and she was afraid to leave the World of the Gods and wished she could get back her shape again. She flew to Midyir and buzzed round him, but he was making a brightness on the Earth and did not hear her; when she lit on his hand he brushed her away.

She went to Angus, and he was making music on the strings of his tiompan; when she buzzed about him he said: "You have a sweet song, little fly," and he made the tiompan buzz like a fly. She lit on his hand, and he said: "You are very beautiful, little golden fly, and because you are beautiful I will give you a gift. Now speak and ask for the gift that will please you best."

Then Ethaun was able to speak, and she said:

"O Angus, give me back my shape again. I am Ethaun, and Fuamach has changed me into a fly and bidden me wander till I get back my shape."

Angus looked sadly at the little golden fly, and said:

"It is only in Ildathach that I am a Shape-Changer. Come with me to that land and I will

The Golden Fly

make a palace for you and while you are in it you will have the shape of Ethaun."

" I will go with you," said Ethaun, " and live in your palace."

She went with him, and he brought her into a beautiful palace that had all the colours of the rainbow. It had four windows to it, and when she looked out of the window to the West she saw a great wood of pine trees and oak trees and trees that had golden apples ; when she looked out of the window to the North she saw a great mountain shaped like a spear, and white like flame ; and when she looked to the South she saw a far-stretching plain with many little gleaming lakes ; but the window to the East was fast closed, and Angus said she must never unbar it.

Ethaun was happy for a long time in the rainbow-palace and Angus came and played to her and told her tales of all the worlds ; but at last the old longing came to her and she grew weary of everything she could see.

" I wish the walls of the palace would fall and the trees wither," she said, " for they are always the same ! "

She went to the window in the East and un-barred it. She saw the sea outside it, wind-driven and white with foam, and a great wind blew the window open and caught Ethaun and whirled her out of the palace, and she became again a little golden fly. She wandered and wandered through the World of the Bright Shadow that is called Ildathach till she came to the World of the Dark Shadow that is Earth, and she wandered there for a long time, scorched by the sun and beaten by the rain, till she came to a beautiful house where a king and queen were standing together. The king had a golden cup full of mead and he was giving it to the queen. Ethaun lit on the edge of the cup, but the queen never saw the little golden fly, and she did not know that it slipped into the mead, and she drank it with the mead.

Afterwards there was a child born to the queen—a strange beautiful child, and the queen called her Ethaun. Every one in the palace loved the child and tried to please her but nothing pleased her for long and as she grew older and more beautiful they tried harder to please her but she was never contented. The queen was sad at heart because of this, and the sadness grew on her day by day and she began to think her child was of the Deathless Ones that bring with them too much joy or too much sorrow for mortals.

One day Ethaun said the Queen's singer had no songs worth listening to and she began to sing one of her own songs; as she sang, the queen looked into her eyes and knew that Ethaun was no child of hers, and when she knew it she bowed herself in her seat and died. The king said Ethaun brought ill-luck and he sent her away to live in a little hut of woven branches in a forest where only shepherds and simple people came to her and brought her food.

She grew every day more beautiful and walked

The Golden Fly

under the great trees in the forest and sang her
own songs. One day the king of all Ireland came
riding by. His name was Eochy, and he was
young and beautiful and strong. When he saw
Ethaun he said:

" No woman in the world is beautiful after this
one ! " and he got down from his horse and came
to Ethaun. She was sitting outside the little hut
and combing her hair in the sunshine, and her
hair was like fine gold and very long.

" What is your name ? " said the king, " and
what man is your father ? "

" Ethaun is my name," said she, " and a king
is my father."

" It is wrong," said Eochy, " that your beauty
should be shut in this forest, come with me and
you shall be the High Queen of Ireland."

Then Ethaun looked at Eochy, and it seemed
to her that she had known him always. She said:

" I have waited here for you and no other.
Take me into your house, High King."

Eochy took her with him and made her his
queen, and all the country that he ruled was
glad because the High Queen was so beautiful.
Eochy made a wonderful house for her. It had
nine doors of carved red yew, and precious stones
were in the walls of it. Ethaun and the king lived
in it, and the harpers sang to them, and the noblest
warriors in Erin stood about their doors. The king
was happy, but there was always in the mind of
Ethaun a beauty that made the rich hangings seem
poor and the jewels dull and she had a song in

her heart that took the music out of all other songs.
The harpers of the Five Provinces of Ireland came
into the feast hall of Eochy at Samhain, but there
was weariness on the face of Ethaun while they
played, and though the High King gave them
gold rings and jewels and high seats of honour
they had no joy in coming to his house.

The warriors clashed their swords when the
High Queen passed but any one who looked into
her eyes dreamed of strange countries and had in
him the longing to go over seas, and Eochy was
grieved because the noblest of his chiefs became
like the lonely bird of the waves that never builds
a nest.

One day Ethaun leaned against the carved yew
door of her sunny-palace and watched the sea-
gulls wheeling in the blueness of the sky. Inside,
the Fool was strewing green rushes and scented
leaves and buds before her chair. The Fool was
always in the palace because his wits had gone
from him, and people say that fools have the dark
wisdom of the gods. Ethaun could hear him
singing :

" I had a black hound and a white.
The Day is long, and long the Night.

A great wave swallowed up the sea,
And still the hounds were following me.

The white hound had a crown of gold,
But no one saw it, young or old.

The Golden Fly

The black hound's feet were swift as fire—
'Tis he that was my heart's desire.

The Sun and Moon leaned from the sky
When I and my two hounds went by."

Ethaun turned from the door and went into
the room where the Fool was. Her dress swept
the young green leaves but she had no thought
of them or of the little flowers the Fool had
put with the rushes.

" Go on singing ! " she said. " I wish my heart
were as lightsome as yours."

" How could your heart be lightsome, Queen,"
said the Fool, " when you will not give the
flower a chance to blossom, or the hound a chance
to catch his prey, or the bird a clear sky to sing
in ? If you were of the Deathless Ones you would
burn the world to warm your hands ! "

The redness of shame spread itself in Ethaun's
face. She stooped and lifted a little bud from the
floor.

" I think the Deathless Ones could make this
bud blossom," she said, " but all the buds that I
break off wither in my hands. I will break no
more buds, Fool."

While she spoke there was a noise outside, and
Ethaun asked her women what it was.

" Only a beggar-man they are driving away.
He says he is a juggler and can do tricks."

" Let him stay," said Ethaun, " and I will see
his tricks."

"O Queen," said the women, "he is a starveling and ignorant; how could he please you when Incar, the King's juggler, did not please you?"

"Let the man stay," said Ethaun; "if he has the will to please me he will please—and to-night Incar will please me too."

She stepped out through the carved yew door and bade the beggar-man do his tricks. He was clumsy and his tricks were not worth looking at, but the Queen gave him a ring from her finger and the little bud she had in her hand, and said:

"Stay here to-night and the King's juggler will teach you good feats."

The beggar-man put the ring in his bosom but he kept the bud in his hands and suddenly it blossomed into a rose and he plucked the petals apart and flung them into the air and they became beautiful white birds and they sang till every one forgot the sky above them and the earth beneath them with gladness, but Ethaun put her hands before her eyes and the tears came through her fingers.

The birds circled away into the air, singing, and when the people looked for the beggar-man he was gone. Ethaun called after him: "Angus! Angus! Come back!" but no one answered, and there was only the far-off singing of the birds.

That night the King's juggler did feats with golden balls and with whirling swords and Ethaun praised him so that for gladness he thought of new feats, and while the people were shouting with

The Golden Fly

delight a tall dark man in the robes of a foreigner came into the hall. Now the king loved to speak with men from far countries and he called the stranger to him, and said:

"What knowledge have you, and what skill is in your fingers?"

"I know," said the stranger, "where the sun goes when the earth does not see it, and I have skill in the playing of chess."

Gladness was on the king when he heard of the chess-playing, for he himself had such skill that no one could beat him.

"I will play a game with you," he said. "Let the chess-board be brought."

"O King," said the attendants, "there is only the Queen's chess-board, and it is locked away because she said it was not beautiful."

"I will go myself for the board," said the king, and he rose up to get it.

The stranger brought out a chess-board that had the squares made of precious stones brighter than any stones of the earth and he set the men on it. They were of gold and ivory, but the ivory was whiter than the whiteness of a cloud and the gold brighter than the sunset.

"I will give you this board in exchange for yours," he said to the queen.

"No," said Ethaun, "the board that Eochy made for me I will keep."

"I will make something for you, too," said the stranger. "I will make worlds for you."

Ethaun looked into his eyes, and she remembered

the World of the Gods, and Midyir, and Angus, and Fuamach, and how she had been a little golden fly.

"O Midyir," she said, "in all the worlds I would be nothing but a little fly. I have wandered far, but I have learned wisdom at last from a Fool. I am going to make a world for myself."

As she was speaking Eochy came back with the board.

"The first games on my board," said Midyir, "the last on yours."

"Be it so," said Eochy. Midyir began to set out the men. "What are we playing for?" said Eochy.

"Let the winner decide," said Midyir.

Eochy won the first game, and he asked for fifty horses out of fairyland.

"I will get them," said Midyir, and they played again. Eochy won, and he said:

"I will ask for four hard things. Make a road over Moin Lamraide; clear Mide of stones; cover the district of Tethra with rushes; and the district of Darbrech with trees."

"When you rise in the morning stand on the little hill near your house and you will see all these things done," said Midyir. They played again, and Midyir won.

"What do you ask?" said Eochy.

"I ask Ethaun," said Midyir.

"I will never give her!" said Eochy.

"The horses of fairyland are trampling outside

The Golden Fly

your door, O King," said Midyir, " give me my
asking." And he said to Ethaun : " Will you come
into your own world again ? "

Ethaun said :

" There is no world of all the worlds my own,
for I have never made a place for myself, but
Eochy has made a place for me and all the people
have brought me gifts, and for the space of a
year I will stay with them and bring them gladness."

" I will come at the year's end," said Midyir,
and he left the hall, but no man saw him
go.

After that there was never such a year in
Ireland. The three crowns were on the land—
a crown of plenty, a crown of victory, and a crown
of song. Ethaun gave gifts to all the High King's
people, and to Eochy she gave a gladness beyond
the dream of a man's heart when it is fullest ;
and at Samhain time Eochy made a great feast
and the kings of Ireland and the poets and the
druids were there, and gladness was in the heart
of every one.

Suddenly there was a light in the hall that
made the torches and the great candles that are
lit only for kings' feasts burn dim, and Midyir the
Red-Maned, stood in the hall. Then the ollavs
and the poets and the druids and chiefs bowed
themselves, and the king bowed himself, because
Midyir had come. Midyir turned his eyes to
where Ethaun sat in a seat of carved silver by the
king. He had a small cruit such as musicians

carry and he made a sweet music on it and sang :

Come with me ! Come with me ! Ethaun,
Leave the weary portals of life, leave the doon,
*   leave the bawn.*
*   Come ! Come ! Come ! Ethaun.*
Lo ! the white-maned untamable horses, out-racing
*   the wind,*
Scatter the embers of day as they pass, and the
*   riders who bind*
The suns to their chariot wheels and exult are
*   calling your name,*
Are calling your name through the night, Ethaun,
*   and the night is a-flame,*
*   Ethaun ! Ethaun ! Ethaun !*
Come with us, Ethaun, to Moy-Mell where the
*   star-flocks are straying*
Like troops of immortal birds for ever delaying,
*   delaying*
The moment of flight that would take them away
*   from the honey-sweet plain.*
Surely you long for waves that break into starry rain
And are fain of flowers that need not die to blossom
*   again.*
Why have you turned away from me your only lover ?
What lure have you seen in the eyes of a mortal
*   that clay must cover ?*
Come back to me ! come back, Ethaun ! The
*   high-built heavenly places*
Mourn for you, and the lights are quenched, and
*   for you immortal faces*

The Golden Fly

Grow wan as faces that die. O Flame-Fair
    Swan of Delight,
Come with me, leave the weary portals of sleep-
    heavy Night ;
The hosts are waiting, their horses trample the
    ashes of day ;
Come, Light of a World that is Deathless, come
    away ! Come away !

Midyir stretched his hands to Ethaun, and she turned to Eochy and kissed him.

"I have put into a year the gladness of a long life," she said, "and to-night you have heard the music of Faery, and echoes of it will be in the harp-strings of the men of Ireland for ever, and you will be remembered as long as wind blows and water runs, because Ethaun—whom Midyir loved—loved you."

She put her hand in Midyir's and they rose together as flame rises or as the white light rises in the sky when it is morning ; and in the World of the Gods Angus waited for them, and Fuamach ; and they walked together again as they had walked from the beginning of time.

THE CHILDREN OF LIR

ONG ago when the Tuatha De Danaan lived in Ireland there was a great King called Lir. He had four children—Fionnuala, Aodh, Fiacra, and Conn. Fionnuala was the eldest and she was as beautiful as sunshine in blossomed branches ; Aodh was like a young eagle in the blue of the sky ; and his two brothers, Fiacra and Conn, were as beautiful as running water.

In those days sorrow was not known in Ireland : the mountains were crowned with light, and the lakes and rivers had strange starlike flowers that shook a rain of jewelled dust on the white horses of the De Danaans when they came down to drink. The horses were swifter than any horses that are living now and they could go over the waves of the sea and under deep lake-water without hurt to themselves. Lir's four children had each one a white horse and two hounds that were whiter than snow.

Every one in Lir's kingdom loved Fionnuala, and Aodh, and Fiacra, and Conn, except their

145

Celtic Wonder-Tales

step-mother, Aoifa. She hated them, and her hatred pursued them as a wolf pursues a wounded fawn. She sought to harm them by spells and witchcraft. She took them in her chariot to the Lake of Darvra in Westmeath. She made them bathe in the lake and when they were coming out of the water she struck them with a rod of enchantment and turned them into four white swans.

" Swim as wild swans on this lake," she said, " for three hundred years, and when that time is ended swim three hundred years on the narrow sea of the Moyle, and when that time is ended swim three hundred years on the Western Sea that has no bounds but the sky."

Then Fionnuala, that was a swan, said:

" O Wicked Woman, a doom will come upon you heavier than the doom you have put on us and you will be more sorrowful than we are to-day. And if you would win any pity in the hour of your calamity tell us now how we may know when the doom will end for us."

"The doom will end when a king from the North weds a queen from the South ; when a druid with a shaven crown comes over the seas ; when you hear the sound of a little bell that rings for prayers."

The swans spread their wings and flew away over the lake. They made a very sorrowful singing as they went, lamenting for themselves.

When the Great King, their father, knew the sorrow that had come to him, he hastened down to the shore of the lake and called his children.

146

The Children of Lir

They came flying to him, four white swans, and he said:

"Come to me, Fionnuala; come Aodh; come Conn; come Fiacra." He put his hands on them and caressed them and said: "I cannot give you back your shapes till the doom that is laid on you is ended, but come back now to the house that is mine and yours, White Children of my Heart."

Then Fionnuala answered him:

"The shadow of the woman who ensnared us lies on the threshold of your door: we cannot cross it."

And Lir said:

"The woman who ensnared you is far from any home this night. She is herself ensnared, and fierce winds drive her into all the restless places of the earth. She has lost her beauty and become terrible; she is a Demon of the Air, and must wander desolate to the end of time—but for you there is the firelight of home. Come back with me."

Then Conn said:

"May good fortune be on the threshold of your door from this time and for ever, but we cannot cross it, for we have the hearts of wild swans and we must fly in the dusk and feel the water moving under our bodies; we must hear the lonesome cries of the night. We have the voices only of the children you knew; we have the songs you taught us—that is all. Gold crowns are red in the firelight, but redder and fairer is dawn."

147

Lir stretched out his hands and blessed his children. He said:

" May all beautiful things grow henceforth more beautiful to you, and may the song you have be melody in the heart of whoever hears it. May your wings winnow joy for you out of the air, and your feet be glad in the water-ways. My blessing be on you till the sea loses its saltness and the trees forget to bud in springtime. And farewell, Fionnuala, my white blossom; and farewell Aodh, that was the red flame of my heart; and farewell, Conn, that brought me gladness; and farewell, Fiacra, my treasure. Lonesome it is for you, flying far off in places strange to you; lonesome it is for me without you. Bitter it is to say farewell, and farewell, and nothing else but farewell."

Lir covered his face with his mantle and sorrow was heavy on him, but the swans rose into the air and flew away calling to each other. They called with the voices of children, but in their heart was the gladness of swans when they feel the air beneath them and stretch their necks to the freedom of the sky.

Three hundred years they flew over Lake Darvra and swam on its waters. Often their father came to the lake and called them to him and caressed them; often their kinsfolk came to talk with them; often harpers and musicians came to listen to the wonder of their singing. When three hundred years were ended the swans rose suddenly and flew far and far away. Their

The Children of Lir

father sought them, and their kinsfolk sought them, but the swans never touched earth or rested once till they came to the narrow Sea of the Moyle that flows between Ireland and Scotland. A cold stormy sea it was, and lonely. The swans had no one to listen to their singing, and little heart for singing amid the green curling bitter waves. The storm-wind beat roughly on them, and often they were separated and calling to one another without hope of an answer. Then Fionnuala, for she was the wisest, said :

" Let us choose a place of meeting, so that when we are separated and lost and wandering each one will know where to wait for the others.

The swans, her brothers, said it was a good thought ; they agreed to meet together in one place, and the place they chose was Carraig-na-Ron, the Rock of the Seals. And it was well they made that choice, for a great storm came on them one night and scattered them far out over the sea. Their voices were drowned in the tempest and they were driven hither and thither in the darkness.

In the pale morning Fionnuala came to the Rock of the Seals. Her feathers were broken with the wind and draggled with the saltness of the sea and she was lamenting and calling on Aodh and Fiacra and Conn.

" O Conn, that I sheltered under my feathers, come to me ! O Fiacra, come to me ! O Aodh, Aodh, Aodh, come to me ! "

And when she did not see them, and no voice answered, she made a sore lamentation and said:

"O bitter night that was blacker than the doom of Aoifa at the first to us! O three that I loved! O three that I loved! The waves are over your heads and I am desolate!"

She saw the red sun rising, and when the redness touched the waters, Conn came flying to her. His feathers were broken with the wind and draggled with the saltness of the sea. Fionnuala gathered him under her wings and comforted him, and she said:

"The day would not seem bitter to me now if only Aodh and Fiacra were come."

In a little while Fiacra came to her over the rough sea. She sheltered and comforted him with her wings, and she cried over the waters:

"O Aodh, Aodh, Aodh, come to me!"

The sun was high in the heavens when Aodh came, and he came with his feathers bright and shining and no trace of the bitter storm on him.

"O where have you been, Aodh?" said Fionnuala and Fiacra and Conn to him.

"I have been flying where I got sight of our kinsfolk. I have seen the white steeds that are swifter than the winds of March, and the riders that were comrades to us when we had our own shapes. I have seen Aodh and Fergus, the two sons of Bove Dearg."

"O tell us, Aodh, where we may get sight of them!" said the swans.

The Children of Lir

" They are at the river mouth of the Ban,"
said Aodh, " Let us go there, and we may see
them though we cannot leave the Moyle."

So much gladness came on all the swans that
they forgot their weariness and the grievous
buffeting of the storm and they rose and flew
to the river mouth of the Bann. They saw their
kinsfolk, the beautiful company of the Faery
Host, shining with every colour under heaven
and joyous as the wind in Springtime.

" O tell us, dear kinsfolk," said the swans,
" how it is with our father ? "

" The Great King has wrapped his robes of
beauty about him, and feasts with those from
whom age cannot take youth and light-hearted-
ness," said Fergus.

" Ah," said Fionnuala, " he feasts and it is
well with him ! The joy-flame on his hearth
cannot quench itself in ashes. He cannot hear
us calling through the night—the wild swans,
the wanderers, the lost children."

The Faery Host was troubled, seeing the piteous
plight of the swans, but Aodh, that was a
swan said to Fergus, his kinsman and comrade :

" Do not cloud your face for us, Fergus ;
the horse you ride is white, but I ride a whiter—
the cold curling white wave of the sea."

Then Fiacra said :

" O Fergus, does my own white horse forget
me, now that I am here in the cold Moyle ? "

And Conn said :

"O Fergus, tell my two hounds that I will come back to them some day."

The memory of all beautiful things came on the swans, and they were sorrowful, and Fionnuala said:

"O beautiful comrades, I never thought that beauty could bring sorrow: now the sight of it breaks my heart," and she said to her brothers: "Let us go before our hearts are melted utterly."

The swans went over the Moyle then, and they were lamenting, and Fionnuala said:

"There is joy and feasting in the house of Lir to-night, but his four children are without a roof to cover them."

"It is a poor garment our feathers make when the wind blows through them: often we had the purple of kings' children on us.

"We are cold to-night, and it is a cold bed the sea makes: often we had beds of down with broidered coverings.

"Often we drank mead from gold cups in the house of our father; now we have the bitterness of the sea and the harshness of sand in our mouths.

"It is weariness—O a great weariness—to be flying over the Moyle; without rest, without companions, without comfort.

"I am thinking of Angus to-night: he has the laughter of joy about him for ever.

"I am thinking to-night of Mananaun, and of white blossoms on silver branches.

"O swans, my brothers, I am thinking of beauty, and we are flying away from it for ever."

The Children of Lir

The swans did not see the company of the
Faery Host again. They swam on the cold
stormy sea of the Moyle, and they were there
till three hundred years were ended.

"It is time for us to go," said Fionnuala,
"we must seek the Western Sea."

The swans shook the water of the Moyle from
their feathers and stretched out their wings to
fly.

When they were come to the Western Sea
there was sorrow on them, for the sea was wilder
and colder and more terrible than the Moyle.
The swans were on that sea and flying over it
for three hundred years, and all that time they
had no comfort, and never once did they hear
the foot-fall of hound or horse or see their
faery kinsfolk.

When the time was ended, the swans rose out
of the water and cried joyfully to each other:
"Let us go home now, the time is ended!"

They flew swiftly, and yet they were all day
flying before they came to the place where
Lir had his dwelling; when they looked down
they saw no light in the house, they heard no
music, no sound of voices. The many-coloured
house was desolate and all the beauty was gone
from it; the white hounds and the bright-
maned horses were gone, and all the beautiful
glad-hearted folk of the Sidhe.

"Every place is dark to us!" said Conn.
"Look at the hills!"

The swans looked at the hills they had known,

and every hill and mountain they could see was dark and sorrowful: not one had a star-heart of light, not one had a flame-crown, not one had music pulsing through it like a great breath.

"O Aodh, and Conn, and Fiacra," said Fionnuala, "beauty is gone from the earth: we have no home now!"

The swans hid themselves in the long dank grass, till morning. They did not speak to each other; they did not make a lamentation; they were silent with heaviness of grief. When they felt the light of morning they rose in the air and flew in wide circles seeking their kinsfolk. They saw the dwellings of strangers, and a strange people tending flocks and sowing corn on plains where the Tuatha De Danaan had hunted white stags with horns of silver.

"The grief of all griefs has come upon us!" said Fionnuala. "It is no matter now whether we have the green earth under us or bitter sea-waves: it is little to us now that we are in swans' bodies."

Her brothers had no words to answer her; they were dumb with grief till Aodh said:

"Let us fly far from the desolate house and the dead hills. Let us go where we can hear the thunder of the Western Sea."

The swans spread their wings and flew westward till they came to a little reedy lake, and they alit there and sheltered themselves, for they had no heart to go farther.

They took no notice of the days and often

The Children of Lir

they did not know whether it was the moon or the sun that was in the sky, but they sang to each other, and that was all the comfort they had.

One day, while Fionnuala was singing, a man of the stranger-race drew near to listen. He had the aspect of one who had endured much hardship. His garments were poor and ragged. His hair was bleached by sun and rain. As he listened to the song a light came into his eyes and his whole face grew beautiful. When the song ended he bowed himself before the swans and said:

"White Swans of the Wilderness, ye have flown over many lands. Tell me, have ye seen aught of Tir-nan-Oge, where no one loses youth; or Tir-na-Moe, where all that is beautiful lives for ever; or Moy-Mell, that is so honey-sweet with blossom?"

"Have we seen Tir-nan-Oge? It is our own country! We are the children of Lir the King of it."

"Where is that country? How may one reach it? Tell me!"

"Ochone! It is not anywhere on the ridge of the world. Our father's house is desolate!"

"Ye are lying, to make sport for yourselves! Tir-nan-Oge cannot perish—rather would the whole world fall to ruin!

"O would we had anything but the bitterness of truth on our tongues!" said Aodh. "Would we could see even one leaf from those trees with shining branches where the many-coloured

155

birds used to sing! Ochone! Ochone! for all the beauty that has perished with Tir-nan-Oge!"

The stranger cried out a loud sorrowful cry and threw himself on the ground. His fingers tore at the roots of the grass. His body writhed and trembled with grief.

The children of Lir wondered at him, and Aodh said:

"Put away this fierceness of grief and take consolation to yourself. We, with so much heavier sorrow, have not lamented after this fashion."

The stranger raised himself: his eyes blazed like the eyes of a hunted animal when it turns on the hunters.

"How could your sorrow be equal to mine? Ye have dwelt in Tir-nan-Oge; ye have ridden horses whiter than the snow of one night and swifter than the storm-wind; ye have gathered flowers in the Plain of Honey. But I have never seen it—never once! Look at me! I was born a king! I have become an outcast, the laughing stock of slaves! I am Aibric the wanderer!—I have given all—all, for the hope of finding that country. It is gone now—it is not anywhere on the round of the world!"

"Stay with us," said Fiacra, "and we will sing for you, and tell you stories of Tir-nan-Oge."

"I cannot stay with you! I cannot listen to your songs! I must go on seeking; seeking;

seeking while I live. When I am dead my dreams will not torment me. I shall have my fill of quietness then."

"Can you not believe us when we tell you that Tir-nan-Oge is gone like the white mists of morning ? It is nowhere."

"It is in my heart, and in my mind, and in my soul ! It burns like fire ! It drives me like a tireless wind ! I am going. Farewell !

"Stay !" cried Aodh, "we will go with you. There is nothing anywhere for us now but brown earth and drifting clouds and wan waters. Why should we not go from place to place as the wind goes, and see each day new fields of reeds, new forest trees, new mountains ? O, we shall never see the star-heart in any mountain again !"

"The mountains are dead," said Conn.

"The mountains are not dead," said Aibric. "They are dark and silent, but they are not dead. I know. I have cried to them in the night and laid my forehead against theirs and felt the beating of their mighty hearts. They are wiser than the wisest druid, more tender than the tenderest mother. It is they who keep the world alive."

"O," said Fionnuala, "if the mountains are indeed alive let us go to them ; let us tell them our sorrowful story. They will pity us and we shall not be utterly desolate."

Aibric and the swans journeyed together, and at dusk they came to a tall beautiful mountain— the mountain that is called Nephin, in the West.

It looked dark and sombre against the fading sky, and the sight of it, discrowned and silent, struck chill to the hearts of our wild swans : they turned away their heads to hide the tears in their eyes. But Aibric stretched his hands to the mountain and cried out:

"O beautiful glorious Comrade, pity us! Tir-nan-Oge is no more, and Moy-Mell is lost for ever! Welcome the children of Lir, for we have nothing left but you and the earth of Ireland!"

Then a wonder happened.

The star-heart of Nephin shone out— magnificent—tremulous—coloured like a pale amethyst.

The swans cried out to each other:

"The mountain is alive! Beauty has come again to the earth! Aibric, you have given us back the Land of Youth!"

A delicate faery music trembled and died away and was born again in the still evening air, and more and more the radiance deepened in the heart of Nephin. The swans began to sing most sweetly and joyously, and at the sound of that singing the star-heart showed in mountain after mountain till every mountain in Ireland pulsed and shone.

"Crown yourselves, mountains!" said Aodh, "that we may know the De Danaans are still alive and Lir's house is builded now where old age cannot wither it!"

The mountains sent up great jewelled rays of

The Children of Lir

light so that each one was crowned with a rainbow; and when the Children of Lir saw that splendour they had no more thought of the years they had spent over dark troublous waters, and they said to each other :

" Would we could hear the sound of the little bell that rings for prayers, and feel our swan-bodies fall from us ! "

" I know the sound of a bell that rings for prayers," said Aibric, " and I will bring you where you can hear it. I will bring you to Saint Kemoc and you will hear the sound of his bell."

" Let us go," said the swans, and Aibric brought them to the Saint. The Saint held up his hands and blessed God when he saw them, and he besought them to remain a while and to tell him the story of their wanderings. He brought them into his little church and they were there with him in peace and happiness relating to him the wonders of the Land of Youth. It came to pass then that word reached the wife of King Largnen concerning the swans : she asked the king to get them for her, and because she demanded them with vehemence, the king journeyed to the Church of Saint Kemoc to get the swans.

When he was come, Saint Kemoc refused to give him the swans and Largnen forced his way into the church to take them. Now, he was a king of the North, and his wife was a queen of the South, and it was ordained that such a king should put an end to the power of Aoifa's spell.

He came to the altar, and the swans were close to it. He put his hands on the swans to take them by force. When he touched them the swan-feathers dwindled and shrivelled and became as fine dust, and the bodies of Lir's children became as a handful of dust, but their spirits attained to freedom and joined their kinsfolk in the Land-of-the-Ever-Living.

It was Aibric who remembered the story of the children of Lir, because he loved them. He told the story to the people of Ireland, and they were so fond of the story and had such pity for Lir's children that they made a law that no one was to hurt a wild swan, and when they saw a swan flying they would say:

"My blessing with you, white swan, for the sake of Lir's children!"

THE LUCK-CHILD

IDAN, Osric, and Teigue, were the cow-herds of Eterscel, the High King of Ireland. Aidan was old and gentle, Osric was young and fierce, Teigue was an omadhaun—a fool—they watched the cattle of the king and chased the wild beasts from them. At night they slept in little wicker huts on the edge of the forest.

One day as Teigue was gathering dry sticks for his fire he saw a very young child lying wrapped in a mantle at the foot of a pine tree. He went over to the child and it smiled in his face. He left off gathering sticks and sat down beside it. Osric came to see what was keeping Teigue.

" A fool's errand is long a-doing," he said. " What are you loitering here for, when the meat is waiting for the fire and the fire is waiting for the sticks ? "

" I have here," said Teigue, " what is better than meat, a gift from the Hidden People."

Osric looked at the child.

" We have little use for a nine-months' infant," he said.

The child smiled at him.

"Where could we keep it?" he asked Teigue.

"I will make a house for it," said Teigue, "a little house in the middle of the forest, that no one can find but myself."

"'Tis a pity the child should perish in the forest," said Osric. "Of a truth the house must be built."

Aidan came. He lifted the child in his arms and looked at the mantle wrapped about it. The mantle was thickly embroidered with gold flowers.

"This is the child of some queen," he said. "One day great folk will come seeking her."

"I will not let the great folk take her away," said Teigue. "She is my Luck-Child. She is Osric's Luck-Child too, and we are going to make a house for her, and she will bring us good luck every day of our lives."

"She is my Luck-Child too," said Aidan. "We three will make a secret house in the forest, and there we will keep her from prying eyes."

They sought out a place, a hidden green spot in the forest. They made a house, and there they nurtured the child in secret. Year by year she throve and grew with them. Teigue brought her berries and taught her to play on a little reed flute. When she made music on it the wild creatures of the woods came about her. She played with the spotted fawns, and the king of the wolves crouched before her and licked her hands. Osric made a bow for her, and taught her how to shoot with arrows, but she had no wish

The Luck-Child

to kill any beast, for all the forest-creatures were her friends. Aidan told her stories. He told her how the sun changed into a White Hound at night, and Lugh the Long-Handed put a silver chain on it and led it away to his Secret Palace, and it crouched at his feet till the morning, when he loosed it and let it run through the sky again. He told her how Brigit counted the stars so that no littlest one got lost, and how she hurried them away in the morning before Lugh's great hound came out to frighten them. He said that Brigit came in the very early mornings to gather herbs of healing, for it was she who gave the secret of healing to wise physicians, and it was she gave power and virtue to every herb that grows. He said that once the High King's Poet had seen Brigit and had made a song about her and called her 'The Pure Perpetual Ashless Fire of the Gael.'

The Luck-Child loved to hear Aidan's stories. She loved them even when she had grown quite tall and wise and was no longer a child.

Teigue was sorry that she grew up so quickly. He sat down one day and began to lament and cry Ochone! about it.

" Why are you lamenting and crying Ochone ? " said Osric.

" Because my Luck-Child has grown up and the Hidden People will see that she is no longer a child. They will take her and make her a queen amongst them, and she will never come back to us. Ochone! Ochone! "

165

Celtic Wonder-Tales

"If the chiefs and warriors of King Eterscel do not see her," said Osric, "she is safe enough: and if they do come to take her I will not let her go without a fight."

Aidan heard them talking.

"Do not speak of trouble or sorrow when you speak of the Luck-Child," he said. "One day she will come to her own, and then she will give each of us his heart's wish."

"I will wish for a robe all embroidered with gold," said Teigue. "What will you wish for, Osric?"

"For a shield and spear and the right to go into battle with warriors."

"What will you wish for, Aidan?"

"I will wish, O Teigue, to sit in the one dun with the Luck-Child, and hear the poets praising her."

"I will go and tell the Luck-Child our wishes," said Teigue, "so that she may know when she comes to her own."

He ran to the little hut in the forest, and the Luck-Child came out to meet him. She laughed to hear of the wishes, and said she would have a wish herself in the day of good fortune, and it would be to have Teigue, Osric, and Aidan, always with her. She took a little reed flute and began to play on it.

"Listen now," she said to Teigue, "and I will play you music I heard last night when the wind swept down from the hills."

Teigue sat under a pine tree and listened.

166

The Luck-Child

A great white hound came through the wood, and when it saw Teigue it stood and bayed. The hound had a gold collar set with three crystal stones.

"O my Luck-Child," said Teigue, "a king will come after this hound. Go quickly where he can get no sight of you."

She had the will to go, but the hound bayed about her feet and would not let her move. A clear voice called the hound, and through the trees came the High King of Ireland : there was no one with him but his foster-brother.

The king had the swiftness and slenderness of youth on him. 'Tis he that was called the Candle of Beauty in Tara of the Kings—and nowhere on the yellow-crested ridge of the world could his equal be found for hardiness and high-heartedness and honey-sweet wisdom of speech.

His foster-brother had a thick twist of red gold in his hair, and he was the son of a proud northern king. The Luck-Child seemed to both of them a great wonder.

"What maiden is this ? " said the king, and stood looking at her.

"She is my Luck-Child, O King," said Teigue.

"She is no child of thine ! " said the king's foster-brother.

"She is a child of the Hidden People," said Teigue, "and she has brought me luck every day since I found her."

"Tell me," said the king, "how you found her."

"I found her under a pine tree, a nine-months'

child wrapped in a mantle all sewn over with little golden flowers. She is my Luck-Bringer since that day."

"She is mine to-day!" said the king. "O Luck-Child," he said, "will you come and live in my palace and bring me good fortune? It is you will be the High Queen of Ireland, and you will never have to ask a thing the second time."

"Will you give Teigue a gold-embroidered robe and let him stay always with me?"

"I will do that," said the king.

"Will you give Osric a sword and let him go into battle like a warrior?"

"Who is Osric?"

"It was Osric who built the house for me and taught me to shoot with arrows and speared salmon in the rivers for me. I will not go with you without Osric."

"I will give Osric what you ask," said the king, "let him come to me."

"I will bring him," said Teigue, and he ran to find Osric and Aidan.

"O Foster-Brother," said the king, "it is well we lost our way in the woods, for now I have found the queen the druids promised me. 'Good luck,' said they, 'will come to King Eterscel when he weds a queen of unknown lineage.' It is this maiden who will bring me luck."

He took the Luck-Child by the hand, and they went through the wood with the hound following them.

The Luck-Child

Soon they met Teigue, Osric, and Aidan, coming together. The Luck-Child ran to them and brought them to the king.

"Here is Osric," she said, "and Aidan who told me stories."

"I will give Osric one of my own war-chariots and his choice of weapons," said the king. "What am I to give to Aidan?"

"Is there a carved seat in your palace where he can sit and listen to your poet who made the song about Brigit?"

"There are many carved seats in my palace, and he shall sit in one," said Eterscel. "All the three shall sit in seats of honour, for they will be the Foster-Fathers of the High Queen of Ireland."

He turned to the three cow-herds.

"On the day ye built the little hut in the forest for your nurseling ye built truth into the word of my druids, and now I will build honour into your fortune. Ye shall rank with chiefs and the sons of chiefs. Ye shall drink mead in feast-halls of your own, and while I live ye shall have my goodwill and protection."

"May honour and glory be with you for ever, O King," said Aidan. "In a good hour you have come to us."

"We are all going to the palace," said the Luck-Child. "Teigue, where is your flute?"

"It is in the little hut," said Teigue. "I will go back for it."

"Nay," said the king, "there are flutes enough

in the palace! I will give you one of silver, set with jewels."

The Luck-Child clapped her hands for joy.

" I love you," she said to the king. " Come, let us go!"

She took Teigue by the one hand and the king by the other, and they all went to the palace. Every one wondered at the Luck-Child, for since the days of Queen Ethaun, who came out of Fairyland, no one so beautiful was seen in Ireland. The king called her Ethaun, and all the people said that in choosing her he had done well.

There was feasting and gladness on the day they swore troth to each other, and Teigue said the sun got up an hour earlier in the morning and stayed an hour later in the sky that night for gladness.

CONARY MOR

HE night that Conary was born, strange sweet music sounded on all the hills and valleys of Ireland. His mother heard it, and said that Conary must be laid a little while on the green earth that his kinsfolk might own him. He was laid on the green earth, and Dana, the mother of the stars, spread her mantle over him. Then the people of Faery that dwell in the Land of Heart's Desire and in the Land of the Silver Fleece and in the Land That Is Under The Sea came about him, and each one tied a knot of good luck in the fringes of Dana's mantle. The child was brought back to his mother, Ethaun the wife of King Eterscel.

She sent for her husband, and said:

"High King of Ireland, take into your arms the child of the three gifts. He will hear the music in the heart of silence; he will see the Hidden People; he will have the gift of judgment."

Conary was nurtured in three households—in the household of the High King, in the house-

hold of his mother's fosterers, and in the household
of the honey-worded Maunya's of the West.
Five comrades he had that were nurtured with
him, the five grandsons of Donn Dessa, the
Champion—Fer Le, Fer Gar, Fer Rogain, Fer
Gel, and Lomna Druth the Fool, the boys were
named. Conary loved Fer Le, Fer Gar, and Fer
Rogain with a great love. They grew up together
and shared all that they had. Conary's mother
sent him a mantle wrought about the edge and
fringed with gold and a chair carved with strange
devices. He put the mantle by turns on the
three boys and on himself and they sat by turns
in the chair: so they grew up till King Eterscel died.

The druids and chiefs consulted as to who
should be king.

"Let it be Conary," said some, "for he is
beautiful and wise and brave."

Others said: "Conary is no child of King
Eterscel; his mother is of the People of Faery,
and of a surety his father is beautiful and deathless, a king of the Host of the Sidhe. Let the
Bull-Feast be made and the Spell of Truth
spoken that we may know what king to choose."

A black bull was slain, and Aodh the Seer
wrapped himself in the hide. The druids made a
charmed space about him and put the Spell of
Truth upon him that in sleep he might see the
king. Conary's foster brothers came to him, and
said:

"O Conary, all the warriors flock to the Bull-
Feast; come with us."

Conary Mor

Conary was driving two untried horses in a chariot, and he said :

" Go ye to the feast, and I will follow when I have seen how my horses gallop."

He wheeled his chariot about and shook the reins and sped away from Tara, going to the East. He went so fast that soon he saw far off the rim of the sea, and as he was going through a wide green plain great snow-white birds came suddenly about him circling and circling.   One moment they were snow-white and the next they had every colour of the rainbow in their feathers and the colours kept changing.   Conary had never seen such birds, and he made a cast of his spear at one of them.   The spear did not hit the bird.

" Rein up the horses," he said to the charioteer, " and I will cast again."

When the horses were reined up, the birds circled round the chariot and kept lighting on the pole of it and on the green grass.

" O Conary, born in a happy hour," said the charioteer, " do not cast at the birds, for they have come from the Land of the Ever Young."

But Conary did not hearken to the charioteer, he made another cast with the spear and failed. Then he leaped from the chariot and followed the birds on foot.

" If the spear fails me," he said, " the stone will not fail."

He made a cast with the stone, and the stone failed him.   He followed the birds till they came to the sea and when they touched the water they took their own form and Conary saw before him the strong beautiful terrible warriors of the Faery Hills. They would have cast their spears at Conary, but he who was chief among them protected him, and said:

"Was it not told thee, Conary, that thou shouldst do no evil to thy father's birds? There is not one among them that should not be dear to thee for sake of kinship."

"Never until now was this thing told me!" said Conary

"Small heed hast thou paid to thy mother's counsels, O Conary, else she would have told thee thy geas,* for long have thy father's birds been known to her.

"Hearken now to me. The people have gathered into Tara that Aodh the Seer may tell them who is to be king. He has seen the king, a naked youth with a sling and a stone, coming to Tara. Even now chiefs and kings are hastening out on every road that leads to Tara with chariots and gold embroidered raiment for that youth.

"Throw off thy garments of foolishness and hearken to me. Thou art the king appointed, and never since the world began has a king so happy-born come into Ireland. The mountains are glad at thy coming; the rivers and lakes are glad; the forests and green flowery places are glad. Thy kinsfolk are glad. No bitter wind will blow while thou art king: sweet as music will be

* Geas—tabu.

the voice of man to man ; the sun will not hide
from thee ; the stars will not hide from thee ;
thine own folk will not hide from thee until thou
breakest faith.   Nine bonds I put upon thee,
Conary.

Hearken to thy geassa :

It is geas* to let rapine break the peace of thy
reign.

It is geas to go right-hand wise round Tara or
left hand-wise round Bregia.

It is geas to hunt the evil beasts of Cerna.

It is geas to go beyond Tara every ninth night.

It is geas to sleep in a house from which the
light is manifest to outsiders.

It is geas to follow the Three Reds to the
House of Red.

It is geas to let a lone man or a lone woman
come into the same house with thee after sunset.

It is geas to go out of Tara to settle the quarrel
of two kings.

It is geas to let thy drinking-cup be empty of
water.

" These be thy bonds of kingship.   On the
day thou breakest geassa, ruin will come upon
thee.   Keep faith, Conary ! "

The strange warriors vanished, and Conary
fared forth to Tara, naked, as he was bidden.   On
the road by which he went his own foster brothers
were waiting with gold embroidered raiment and
a king's chariot, and right glad they were to bring
him into Tara.

* Geas, pl. geassa—a thing forbidden, a tabu.

Celtic Wonder-Tales

The people acclaimed Conary; the druids and poets acclaimed him; the kings acclaimed him; the earth acclaimed him; so with acclamation and gladness he was made the High King of Ireland.

Never was there any one so beautiful as Conary, never was there such a wonder as his reign. There was peace in the land and peace in the hearts of men so that every one took joy in his fellow. Every husbandman reaped seven harvests. The wolves did not ravage, the frost winds did not bite, and the Hidden Folk came out of the Faery Hills and made music and gladness everywhere.

Beauty and strength increased with Conary year by year, and he might have reigned till Lir's horses go ploughing if his foster brothers had not drawn destruction on him. They were proud and fierce like eagles, and like eagles they longed to take a prey. The good peace that made the reign of Conary wonderful was no joy to them.

In secret they took their weapons and lifted a prey and a spoil, and those from whom they lifted it came to ask for justice of King Conary. But he loved his foster-brothers over-much, with a foolish fondness, and he could not make his face hard against them. He said to those who came for justice:

"Count up your losses and I will give you seven times as much; take it and go hence contented."

Then the foster brothers became like young

Conary Mor

eagles that have tasted blood; they exulted in their fierceness, and raided and drove the prey continually, and other chiefs joined them and raided till the peace that was over Ireland was broken. Now, when that peace was broken the luck of Conary was broken, for it was geas to him to let rapine break the peace of his reign.

There was clamour round the judgment seat of Conary: loud voices cried for the death-sentence on the sons of Donn Dessa.

" I cannot slay my foster-brethren," said the king.

" Cease then to protect them," said the chiefs, " and we will slay them for thee ! "

" I will cease to protect them," said Conary, " but ye shall not slay them ! I will give them ships and the sea-path. Let them draw the death-doom on themselves in other lands : only if they come again to Ireland, slay and spare not ! "

Conary gave his foster-brethren arms and treasures and sent them from him. He took fare-well of them with tears, and to Fer Rogain, whom he loved best, he said :

" O Fer Rogain, I never thought to send thee from me. Though thou hast brought me shame thou wert always my heart's choice and the top-most apple of the tree to me. Thou goest lightly from me now, and there is little sorrow on thee at going."

Fer Rogain said :

" I will have sorrow enough for thee, Conary Mor ; bitter sorrow and tears of blood."

He hardened his face then and went out from the king and got to his ship. All the five got to their ships with their followers. There was no wind, but the rowers rowed till the sea was foaming round the ships. So Conary's foster-brothers left Ireland.

On the high seas they met the battle-ships of Ingcel the One-eyed, a reaver from Britain. Fierce and cruel was the man and terrible in aspect; one eye he had in the middle of his forehead, large as an oxhide, black as a chafer, and with three pupils in it. He was a king's son that was cast out of his own country because of his misdeeds and he had three hundred men in his battle-ships. He made a compact with the five to go raiding in company with them.

"Let us cast lots," said he, "for the country we shall go to first. I will not draw back, though it be the country of my father: nor shall ye draw back, though it be the country of your brother."

They cast lots, and the lot fell on Britain.

They went to that country and drew their ships up on the first good land they sighted and there they made a slaughter and destruction and they burned the dun of the king of that place. In the dun were Ingcel's father and mother and brothers. They perished.

"No destruction will seem grievous to me after this one!" said Ingcel.

The spoil they brought out of that country was rich, and it was divided among them. Then Ingcel said :

Conary Mor

" Raid for raid, let the ships go to Ireland ! "
To Ireland then they turned their ships.

Now, when Conary had banished his foster-
brothers and those other disturbers, there was
quietness, and every one was glad but Conary.
His heart wasted for Fer Le, Fer Gar, and Fer
Rogain, and he took no delight in his royal house
at Tara. Word came to him that two kings in the
south were at variance and he journeyed down
to make peace between them. Now, it was geas
to Conary to settle such a quarrel. He made peace
between the kings and he stayed with them till
ten nights had gone by. This also was geas to
Conary.

Then, because he had broken geassa and loosed
the bonds of his kingship, his Faery kinsfolk
loosed their bonds of protection from him and
their anger showed itself in flames of wizardry
that spread over the hills and covered the plains
of Tara, and in a desolation that blackened the
sky.

Conary saw the flames as he journeyed back
to Tara.

" What is this ? " he said to his warriors.

" It is not hard to tell," said they, " the king's
law has broken down and evil men have made the
land a desolation. Lo ! Tara is burning ! "

But Tara was not burning, and what they saw
were fires of enchantment and wizardry that
consumed nothing but the luck of Conary Mor.

" Let us turn aside," said the king, " and eek
shelter, since our men are not armed for a battle."

Then they wheeled hastily and drove right-hand wise round Tara and left-hand wise round Bregia. This also was geas to Conary.

As they went, three of Conary's white hounds broke their chains of silver and dashed into a thicket where they started a beast. It leaped on the roadway before the chariot of the king—a strange black beast with fiery wrathful eyes; it spat fire at Conary and vanished.

" Alas ! " said the king, " it is one of the beasts of Cerna, and by the nine bonds of my kingship I bound myself not to hunt them. Evil is my fortune this night ! "

They fared heavily along the road of Cualu.

" Whither shall we go to-night," said the king, " and what house will shelter us ? "

" Would that I could tell thee," said Mac Cecht, the Champion. " Often have kings contended for thee : thou hast never sought a shelter till to-night."

" Once I was counted wise," said Conary, " and asked advice from no man. I will go to the Bruiden Da Derga."

" Well I know the great Court of Da Derga," said Mac Cecht ; " nine doors it has, always open to dispense hospitality, and if the king of a district with all his people were to come to it, Da Derga would have guest-rooms and to spare for them. Well hast thou chosen, Conary. I will go before and strike the spark that kindles fire for thee."

Mac Cecht strode forward on the road of Cualu. Huge was he, mountainous and terrible of aspect ;

into the boss of his shield an ox would fit, and
faster than a horse could gallop he strode along
the road of Cualu with mighty earth-shaking
feet.

Heavy then was the heart of Conary and heavy
the hearts of those about him as they fared along
the road. Soon they were aware of three red
horsemen riding before them. Red were the
horses, red the men that rode them, red their
cloaks and armour, all red together.

" Alas," said Conary, " if these three do not
cease to ride before me it needs be I am faring
to my death ! Who will tell them to quit the
roadway ? "

Scarce had Conary spoken the word when his
young son, Le-Fri-Flaith, rode forward. Seven
years were the years of his age and he was the
desire of every eye that looked on him. He was
the candle of beauty at every feast. He was the
little silver branch with white blossoms.

" I will go, my father," Le-Fri-Flaith said,
and he shook the golden bells on his bridle-reins
so that they all rang together.

" Nay," said Conary, " thou art over-young
to go." But the chief druid who rode in the
chariot with Conary, said :

" Let be ; if any one can win obedience from
these riders it is Le-Fri-Flaith, for never in his
life has anything been refused to him, and he is
the dearest and best loved prince in the world."

Conary's son rode after the horsemen. He
came within a spear-cast of them. He could not

gain on them, for swift as he was they were swifter.

"Conary, the High King of Ireland, commands you to leave the road!" he cried to them.

The riders did not swerve aside or slacken speed, but as they rode one turned his head and cried:

"Lo, my son! We are the bearers of dule! We may not stay till we reach the place appointed. Lo, my son!"

Le-Fri-Flaith returned to Conary, and said over those words to him.

"Go after them again," said Conary, "and offer them the gifts of a king, and my protection, if they will leave the road."

Conary's son rode after the horsemen. He came within a spear-cast of them. He could not gain on them, for swift as he was they were swifter.

"Leave the road for the High King of Ireland," he cried, "and ye shall have gifts and a king's protection!"

The riders did not swerve aside or slacken speed, but as they rode one turned his head and cried:

"Lo, my son! We are the bearers of dule! Through ancient enchantment nine shall perish. Lo, my son!"

Le-Fri-Flaith returned to Conary, and said over those words to him.

"Go after them again," said Conary, "offer them double gifts, and my goodwill and protection."

Conary Mor

Conary's son rode after the horsemen. He came within a spear-cast of them. He could not gain on them, for swift as he was they were swifter.

" Leave the road for the High King of Ireland," he cried, " and ye shall have gift upon gift and a king's goodwill and protection ! "

The riders did not swerve aside or slacken speed, but as they rode one turned his head and cried :

" Lo, my son ! We are the bearers of dule ! We are alive and dead. The steeds we ride are from the Faery Hills. They are aweary. Where we go the ravens follow. There will be shields to-night with broken bosses at sun-down. Lo, my son ! "

Le-Fri-Flaith returned to Conary, and said over those words to him.

" Alas ! " said Conary, " of a truth you have spoken with the banished folk, the outcasts from the Faery Hills. Three times they must destroy a king and be themselves destroyed."

They fared behind the horsemen on the road. Then from a wood came forth a fearsome thing, a mis-shapen man with one leg and one arm and one eye ; he had a black pig squealing and twisting on his back, and a hag with a twisted mouth following him. One eye had the hag and one leg and one arm.

" Welcome to Conary," said the swine-carrier ; " long has thy coming been known to us."

" Who art thou," said the king, " and what woman is with thee ? "

"I am Fer Caille, the Man of the Woods. The woman is Cicuil. We bring a black swine for thy feasting lest thou be hungry to-night, for thou art the noblest king that ever came into the world!"

"Some night of my life, Fer Caille, I will taste thy swine; to-night I go to other feasting."

"To-night, O Conary, thou wilt taste my swine, and 'tis my feast will be ready in the house to which thou journeyest."

Foot for foot he kept pace with the king's horses, his ugly wife behind him with her mouth awry and his black pig squealing and twisting on his back.

In this guise they journeyed till they came to the Bruiden Da Derga: and it happened that as Conary was journeying thither along the road of Cualu, his five foster-brothers with Ingcel the One-eyed were heading towards Ben Edar with their ships.

Ingcel sent two men of Erin to stand on the ridge of Ben Edar to spy out a prey, and they saw the train of Conary as it fared along the road of Cualu with the redness of sunset on the spear-blades and chariot wheels.

"A good prey!" said the reavers, and they went back to tell Ingcel that they had seen the chariots and horsemen of Conary, the High King of Ireland.

"Whither do they go?" said Ingcel.

"There is but one house great enough to receive

them, and that is the Bruiden Da Derga," said they. " Not far off is the house."

" I will take it," said Ingcel, " for my share of good luck."

As he spoke there was a loud sharp sound that made the earth tremble ; the ships were hurled backward on the sea ; and fire leaped up, red and ruddy, in the Bruiden.

" What is that ? " asked Ingcel, of Fer Rogain.

" It is the Champion, Mac Cecht, striking a fire of welcome for Conary. Ill-omened is the fire he kindles to-night. Terrible is Mac Cecht, terrible is the king and the folk who befriend him. Let us turn our ships and our hands from Conary and take a prey in the North."

" Never," said Ingcel, " have I turned back from a raid. I saw flames lick the blood of my father, I stepped across the body of my mother, and though Mac Cecht should shake the world-serpent from its hold on the earth I would not go back ! "

He cried to the reavers :

" Let the battle-ships row in to the land ! "

Thrice fifty ships rowed in and were drawn upon the beach. The reavers landed.

Now, when their keels grated on the Irish land the weapons in the Bruiden Da Derga fell to the floor with a scream, and Conary, who had reached the green in front of the Court, paused and listened.

" What sound do you hear ? " said those about him, " beyond the sound of weapons falling ? "

" I hear," said he, " a sound like the keels of my brethren grating on land. Would that indeed to-night they grated on the Irish land, and I might see Fer Rogain and the others again ! "

He passed through the carved door of red yew into the Court, and Da Derga welcomed him, and mead-cups were filled and a feast prepared.

The Bruiden had nine doors and at every door there were seventeen of Conary's chariots. The great road of Cualu ran through the Bruiden and the River Dodder ran through it. The doors were open, and Mac Cecht's fire shone out like the red heart of a mountain when the Faery People are feasting within it.

From the darkness outside came in a lone woman. Evil-looking and hideous, she stood at the door and cried on King Conary.

" What is thy desire, O woman ? " said the king.

" Thine own desire, O King ! " said she.

" Who art thou ? "

" I am Cailb."

" It is no good name," said the king.

" It is no hidden name," said the woman, " and I have many names besides."

Then standing on one foot, with one hand lifted, she chanted in one breath her many names :

" I am Cailb, Samon, Sinand, Seisclend, Sodb, Soegland, Samlocht, Caill, Coll, Dichoem, Dichiuil, Dithim, Dichuimne, Dichruidne, Dairne, Darine, Deruaine, Egem, Egam, Ethamne, Gnim, Cluiche, Cethardam, Nith, Nemain, Noennen,

Conary Mor

Badb, Blose, Bloar, Huae, oe, Aife la Sruth, Mache, Mede, Mod. These be my names, O King!"

"I will call thee by none of them," said Conary, "but say what thou seest for me."

"I see death," said the woman, "and thy flesh in the beaks of ravens."

Mis-shapen and hideous, she stood in the doorway and cast her evil eye on the king and the chiefs about him.

"Leave the doorway," said the king, "food and a gift will be given thee outside."

"Nay," said the woman, "I claim hospitality this night. The Bruiden of Da Derga was built that no one might pass by it shelterless, and never till to-night has any one been driven from the door. If the High King drives me out I will go."

"I do not drive thee out," said Conary, "come through the door."

So, after night-fall into the same house with Conary came a lone woman, and it was geas to him.

When that woman entered the house, Ingcel was holding counsel with the reavers.

"Let each one," he said, "bring a stone and build a cairn. Those who come back alive from the Bruiden will each one lift his stone again, and the stones that remain will be a monument to the dead. I will go to spy out the prey."

Ingcel set out with fifteen men, and the reavers began to build the cairn. The five scions of Donn Dessa lit a great beacon-fire. "It will guide

Ingcel!" they said, but they meant it for Conary.

Ingcel returned, and they all gathered round him.

"What tidings hast thou of the Bruiden?" they asked.

"Royal and kingly is the house, and royal and kingly are the folk within it. My share of luck in the spoils of it."

"Tell us, O Ingcel, what thou sawest within the Bruiden this night.?"

"I saw many guest-places and noble guests, weapons, instruments of music, and golden cups. The first man that I saw when I looked in was large and fair. He had a shield with five golden circles and a five-barbed spear a golden hilted sword at his hand and a brooch of silver in his mantle. About him were nine warriors, all goodly alike, all young and of one appearance. Rods of gold in their mantles, shields of bronze on their arms, ivory-hilted swords beside them. Who are these, Fer Rogain?"

"Well I know them," said Fer Rogain. "The large fair man is Cormac Conloingeas, son of the King of Ulaidh, and the men about him are his nine comrades. Valiant are the champions and valiant is Cormac. They will slay many of the reavers to-night."

"Woe is me!" said Lomna the Fool, "that evil should come to the Bruiden to-night. Well might the place be spared for sake of Cormac!"

"Thy voice is broken, O Lomna," said Ingcel,

" thou art no warrior. Hide thy head. No man shall say of me that I went back from a raid, but let the scions of Donn Dessa go back if they have a mind to it."

" We have sworn an oath to thee," said Fer Rogain, " and while life remains to us we will abide by it."

" Tell us," said Fer Gar, " whom thou sawest ? "

" After that I saw a wondrous champion with a tree of red-gold hair on him. It was curly as a ram's fleece and covered him like a mantle, and though a sackful of red nuts were spilled on his crown not one would fall to the ground but each would stick on the curls and twists and swordlets of that hair. He had a purple tufted cloak on him, and his red shield had plates of gold with rivets of white bronze between the plates. His eyes were of two colours—one black, the other blue. Who is that man, Fer Rogain ? "

" It is Conall Carnach, well-beloved of Conary. That man is a hero among heroes. His shield has shown its gold in many a fight, and his three-ridged spear has brought down many a strong high-headed warrior. He, single-handed, can hold against you seven doors of the Bruiden, and if he chance to come outside he will go through you like a hawk through sparrows or a wolf through sheep, and multitudinous as the stars in heaven will be the fragments of your cloven heads and shattered bones."

" Woe is me," said Lomna the Fool, " that evil should come to Conall Carnach ! If heed were given to me the Destruction would not be wrought to-night ! "

" Clouds of weakness to thee ! " said Ingcel, " thou art no warrior, Lomna."

" Easy is it for thee to speak loud-mouthed," said Lomna, " thou wilt ruin a country not thine own and carry off the head of a king that is a stranger. But woe is me, my head will be the first one lopped this night. It will be tossed among once-kindly spears. Woe is me for Conary ! "

" Next," said Ingcel, " I saw three champions together ; all of them large and fierce of aspect. One had a black shield with ornaments of gold and a cloak flecked with red. His hair was short and brown. The other two had grizzled locks and long black swords. With them was a wondrous spear, a wizard-weapon, plunged in a cauldron of black sleepy liquid. One of the warriors lifted it out, and as he held it by the haft the spear writhed and twisted in his grasp like a living thing and flames ran along the blade so that he was forced to plunge it again in the black liquid. What strange weapon was that, Fer Rogain ? "

" That is the spear brought over the rim of the world for Lugh the Long-Handed. He is the only one who can wield it and he smote the hosts of the Fomor with it and slew Balor of the Evil Eye. Dubthach the Chafer of Ulaidh has the spear. The brown man was Muinremar, son of Seirgind ; the other Sencha, son of Aileel."

" What sawest thou next ? "

Conary Mor

"I saw three fierce mis-shapen ones beside the wall. Big-mouthed and horrible, with grinning teeth."

"Those are the chiefs of the Fomor from the Land of Darkness. They are hostages with Conary lest their people destroy the harvests or molest the flocks and herds. An evil time thy reavers will have when those are loosed against them."

"Woe is me!" said Lomna the Fool, "wise were it to stay the Destruction this night!"

"After that I saw a strange thing, Fer Rogain, "a huge battle-dividing champion with a shield beside him that could hold oceans in its boss. Two bare hills by him and the ridge of a mountain with two lakes. What meant this appearance, Fer Rogain?"

"It is Mac Cecht, the Champion, in his earth-form. Huge is Mac Cecht, terrible is Mac Cecht, an earth-shaker, a tamer of heroes: the bare hills were his knees, the mountain-ridge was his nose, the two lakes were his two eyes. He will break your warriors as a flail breaks corn, they will be threshed in pieces and the ravens will not pick the fragments of their bones out of the sodden ground."

The terror of Mac Cecht fell on the reavers at this word and they went back three ridges: but Ingcel did not go back.

"Tell me," he said to Fer Rogain, "who were the nine beautiful folk with hair outflowing and cloaks about them like silver mist? A ring of gold on each man's thumb; nine rings of crystal on their arms. Gold in their ears, torques of silver round their necks, silver rods in their hands, and above them on the wall nine bags with golden ornaments."

"Those are Conary's harpers: thou hast never heard ought like their harping."

"Woe is me!" said Lomna the Fool, "that they should be scattered to-night! Praise and songs of honour would the man have who would stay the Destruction to-night!"

"I will not go back," said Ingcel.

"Easy for thee to speak loud-mouthed," said Lomna, "thou wilt bring ruin to a country not thine own and carry off the head of a king that is a stranger. Woe is me, my head will be the first one lopped!"

"Mayhap 'tis mine will be the first," said Ingcel.

"Nay," said Lomna the Fool, "thou wilt come safely out of the Destruction, thou and thy brothers, Echell and the Yearling of the Reavers—I foresee it—but I shall be the first to fall. Woe is me!"

"Whom saw you next O Ingcel," said Fer Rogain.

"I saw three youths, beautiful as the harpers, with hair outflowing and mantles of silver mist. In front of each a cup of crystal filled with water, on the water a floating branch of cress."

"Those were three of Conary's nine cup-bearers who go about with him continually. All the nine are from the Faery Hills."

" I saw after that, Fer Rogain, three strange beings. Red they were as the heart of a flame—spectral, awesome—and they sat in a guest-place like folk of honour."

" Those are the banished ones, the bearers of dule, evil-omened. They will slay many to-night, but no man will slay them. They are of the Hidden People, strong and terrible."

" Alas ! " said Lomna the Fool, " Conary is but a dead man if these be in the same house with him to-night ! Woe is me for Conary, the High Noble Flame of the World ! "

Fer Rogain said nothing but he held his cloak before his eyes and his tears wetted it.

" Then," said Ingcel, " I saw a fair young boy seated on a chair of silver with three times fifty youths round him on chairs of silver. He had a cloak on him the colour of an amethyst and a light of three colours was about his head so that his hair looked green and purple and gold. Strange it was to see that young boy. He had fifteen bulrushes in his hand, a thorn at the point of each one, and he was weeping and lamenting where he sat. Who is he, Fer Rogain ? "

It was then Fer Rogain shed tears of blood. He had no voice to answer.

" It is Le-Fri-Flaith," said Lomna, " Conary's son ! Woe is me for Le-Fri-Flaith ! Dear is that young prince to every one that looks on him ! A bosom-solace of warriors, a bough that has blossomed in winter! Woe is me for Le-Fri-Flaith!"

"Then," said Ingcel, "I saw a richly ornamented guest-place hung with curtains of woven silver. Midmost of it was the goodliest man I have ever looked on. His hair was like gold that boils over the melting pot. His face was like the sun on a May morning and his mantle had the changing colours of the day; now it was one colour, now another, and again every colour at once. About his head a wheel of light flashed and pulsed continually. Two warriors were with him, one on either side, white and fair to look on. Who was that man, Fer Rogain?"

"That man was Conary, the noblest of the world's kings. He is without blemish or defect, the joy-bringer, the wise in counsel, the invincible. He, himself, will keep every door of the nine doors to-night. There is none among you that can slay him, nor can anything slay him but thirst, and he will not be without water to-night. What was the High King doing when you looked, Ingcel the One-Eyed?"

"He was sleeping with his feet in the lap of one warrior and his head in the lap of the other. As I looked he started up and said:

"'There is a wind of terror about me! I hear Ossur my hound lamenting.'

"Those beside him said nothing, and he slept and started again. Three times he wakened and said: 'There is a wind of terror about me and a lamentation that quenches laughter; it is

Conary Mor

Ossur my hound.' The third time those beside him said :

" ' It is not your hound that is making lamentation, Conary, but your son.'

" Then Conary sat up wide-eyed and said :

" ' Tulchinne, my juggler, throw up the golden apples and the silver shields and set the bright swords whirling for Le-Fri-Flaith ! '

" Then stepped forward a man in a many-coloured mantle with gold rings in his ears. He had nine shields and nine swords and nine golden apples and he cast them one after the other into the air and kept them whirling and passing each other, rising and falling like bees about their home in a day of Summer. The young prince did not smile to see them, and all at once they clashed together and fell with a scream to the floor. The man with the mantle picked them up. He set them whirling again. Again they screamed and fell to the floor. He picked them up and set them whirling a third time. They screamed and fell.

" ' Never before, O Tulchinne,' said the king, ' has skill failed thee ; why does it fail thee to-night ? '

" ' Good the cause,' said Tulchinne, ' there is an evil thing in front of the Bruiden, a terrible eye regards me from the door.'

" Then that strange young boy that was a-wailing lifted up his face and shook the bul-rushes in his hand towards the door ; fifteen bulrushes he had, and I had fifteen men. Each man lost the sight of his right eye, and a third of my own eye was darkened. Very powerful is that boy, but I will darken his house about him to-night."

"Woe is me," said Lomna the Fool, "the Destruction is come upon us! A wind of keening is before me! Ochone for Conary! Ochone for Le-Fri-Flaith! Ochone for the goodly chiefs that will die to-night!"

"Rise up, my Sea-Wolves," said Ingcel, "and seek your prey!"

They rose up and went forward in the darkness till they spread themselves about the Bruiden Da Derga.

"There are armed men without!" said Conall Carnach and he leaped to his weapons. All the chiefs leaped to their weapons and ran to keep the doors. Lomna the Fool was the first who tried to enter and his head was shorn from him and tossed among the spears. Conall Carnach burst out of the Bruiden and great was the slaughter he made. The reavers brought fire to the walls and carved door-posts of red yew. Three times the flames caught hold and three times those within quenched the fire. The reavers were beaten back, and their men of might and magic consulted together as to what they should do.

"If water were lacking in the Bruiden," they said, "we would have the victory."

Conary Mor

They put a spell on the water. They went again to the attack, and so fierce was the fighting that Conary took his weapons to keep the door. He made the champion's laneway at every door, and the heat and toil of the conflict made him a-thirst.

"Give me to drink!" he cried, and the chief cup-bearer lifted the golden cup that was always full of water for Conary, and lo! it was empty! The water had been poured on the flames. The cup-bearer cried to his fellows: "Give me water from your cups, for the King's cup is empty!"

And lo! their cups were empty too! They sought for water in the stream that went through the Bruiden, the Dodder it was named, and the Dodder was dried up at its fountain-head.

They went to Conary, and said:

"O King, thy cup that was never empty is empty to-night, and there is no water to fill it."

"What Champion will fill my cup to-night?" said the King, and no one answered. Then he cried on Mac Cecht, and Mac Cecht came to him.

"Get me a drink, thou Tamer of Heroes, for thirst consumes me."

"It is not for a little water that I should leave thee, King," said Mac Cecht; "ask a drink of thy cup-bearers."

"My drinking cup is empty," said the King, "and my cup-bearers cannot fill it. Fill it thou, Mac Cecht."

Celtic Wonder-Tales

"If I leave thee, Conary, thou wilt get thy death in this Bruiden."

"I get death now, for thirst like raging fire consumes me."

"Thou shalt have thy drink!" said Mac Cecht, and took the goblet. He cast his eyes round the Bruiden and beheld the son of Conary in his chair of silver. "If there is only one thing saved out of the Bruiden this night it will be Le-Fri-Flaith!" he said: and he took the young prince in his arms and wrapped his mantle closely round him. Under his shield arm he had him, and with his sword bare he went out of the Bruiden.

He made a path for himself through the reavers. He went to the well that was nearest; there was no water in the well. He went to the River Liffey; there was no water in the Liffey. He went to the River Boyne; there was no water in the Boyne. "Hard it is to fill my cup to-night," said Mac Cecht, and he went to the River Shannon; there was no water in the Shannon. He went to every lake and river in Ireland that night, and every lake and river was empty of water. "I will go to my own lake," he said, "it will not hide itself from me to-night!" He went to the Uaran Garad on Magh Ai, and lo! his own lake was empty of water! He searched the lake; he searched it three times over, but he could not find a single drop of water. He was leaving the place when a little bird rose up before him shaking the water from its wings.

Conary Mor

" A blessing be about thee and upon thee for ever little bird, little light above the water, thou hast saved the life of Conary to-night ! " He saw the lake of Uaran Garad, and he filled the drinking cup of Conary with water. The dew came out on the grass again and the whiteness of morning climbed into the sky.

" Look at the good light in the East, Le-Fri-Flaith ! " he said, and drew back the covering mantle from Conary's young son. Le-Fri-Flaith was dead !

Mac Cecht laid the body down on the young grass. He straightened the limbs. He drew the curls of Le-Fri-Flaith's hair through his fingers. " It is seven years to-day since I first saw thee, son of Conary, and never until now did a sight of thee bring grief." He tore boughs from a pine-tree and covered Le-Fri-Flaith from head to foot. Then he took the drinking cup and set his face towards Conary.

Speedy was his going till he reached the Bruiden. It was a desolation that he saw before him. The house was charred and ruined with fire. All the Chiefs had gone from it. The reavers had gone from it. Conary, the king, was lying dead. A wolf prowled by him. Mac Cecht seized the wolf and crushed it with his hands. He lifted up the dead king.

" O Conary," he said, " never believe that Mac Cecht failed thee. Here is the drink."

He poured the water down the throat of Conary.

"Is the drink good, O King?" he said; and out of the other world the voice of Conary answered:

"It is a good drink, Mac Cecht."